HER VOICE WAS A HUSKY, PRIMITIVE INVITATION. . . .

Ruff kissed her deeply. Her mouth was fluid, aggressive. Her lips were pliant, soft and stirring. He wrapped his arms around her and she practically fell against him.

"My knees," she laughed. "I've never been kissed like that."

Ruff didn't quite believe that, but it didn't matter. Her body was against his in the night, her breath was close and warm against his cheek.

"They'll miss us if we're gone too long," Sarah whispered.

"You want to head back?"

"I want to hurry!" she replied. Her eyes were laughing, eager, and Ruff smiled in return as he let his fingers trail off her shoulders and go to the buttons down the front of her dress. . . .

## Wild Westerns From SIGNET

☐ **RUFF JUSTICE #1: SUDDEN THUNDER by Warren T. Long-tree.** (#AE1028—$2.50)*

☐ **RUFF JUSTICE #2: NIGHT OF THE APACHE by Warren T. Longtree.** (#AE1029—$2.50)*

☐ **RUFF JUSTICE #3: BLOOD ON THE MOON by Warren T. Longtree.** (#AE1215—$2.50)*

☐ **RUFF JUSTICE #4: WIDOW CREEK by Warren T. Longtree.** (#AE1422—$2.50)*

☐ **THE TRAILSMAN #1: SEVEN WAGONS WEST by Jon Sharpe.** (#AE1052—$2.25)

☐ **THE TRAILSMAN #2: THE HANGING TRAIL by Jon Sharpe.** (#AE1053—$2.25)

☐ **THE TRAILSMAN #3: MOUNTAIN MAN KILL by Jon Sharpe.** (#AE1130—$2.25)

☐ **THE TRAILSMAN #4: THE SUNDOWN SEARCHERS by Jon Sharpe.** (#AE1158—$2.25)

☐ **THE TRAILSMAN #5: THE RIVER RAIDERS by Jon Sharpe.** (#AE1199—$2.25)

☐ **THE TRAILSMAN #6: DAKOTA WILD by Jon Sharpe.** (#E9777—$2.25)

☐ **THE TRAILSMAN #7: WOLF COUNTRY by Jon Sharpe.** (#E9905—$2.25)

☐ **THE TRAILSMAN #8: SIX-GUN DRIVE by Jon Sharpe.** (#AE1024—$2.25)

*Price slightly higher in Canada

RUFF JUSTICE #4

# *Widow Creek*

*by*

# Warren T. Longtree

A SIGNET BOOK
**NEW AMERICAN LIBRARY**
TIMES MIRROR

## PUBLISHER'S NOTE

This novel is a work of fiction. Names, characters, places, and incidents are either the product of the author's imagination or are used fictiously, and any resemblance to actual persons, living or dead, events, or locales is entirely coincidental.

NAL BOOKS ARE AVAILABLE AT QUANTITY DISCOUNTS WHEN USED TO PROMOTE PRODUCTS OR SERVICES. FOR INFORMATION PLEASE WRITE TO PREMIUM MARKETING DIVISION, THE NEW AMERICAN LIBRARY, INC., 1633 BROADWAY, NEW YORK, NEW YORK 10019.

The first chapter of this book appeared in *Blood on the Moon*, the third volume of this series.

SIGNET TRADEMARK REG. U.S. PAT. OFF. AND FOREIGN COUNTRIES
REGISTERED TRADEMARK—MARCA REGISTRADA
HECHO EN CHICAGO, U.S.A.

SIGNET, SIGNET CLASSICS, MENTOR, PLUME, MERIDIAN AND NAL BOOKS are published by The New American Library, Inc., 1633 Broadway, New York, New York 10019

First Printing, March, 1982

1 2 3 4 5 6 7 8 9

PRINTED IN THE UNITED STATES OF AMERICA

# 1.

THE RIVER WAS a quiet, rambling thing. Black and murmuring beneath starlit skies. The massive oaks along the banks nodded in the silent night breeze as the great paddle-wheeler churned upriver.

Ruff Justice stood at the stern rail, watching the night and the river, which seemed to be made of black silk. The steamboat's paddles stirred up brief, angry ripples of white water, but the night smoothed them over, darkening the waters again.

Not a trace was left of the steamboat's passing. No more trace than a man leaves in his rapid passage across this earth, Justice thought. He turned with a sigh, leaning his back against the rail, listening to the night sounds— the grumbling of frogs along the riverbank, the splashing of the paddle wheels, the vague whispering of the night wind.

He was a tall man, his hair worn long, flowing across his shoulders in dark curls. His mustache drooped beneath the line of his jaw. He was lean, his face a provocative mixture of confidence, contemplation, and coldness.

Just now he wore a dark suit, string tie, and ruffled white shirt. The long-barreled Colt he wore was concealed by his coat flaps.

"Game's up, Mr. Justice!" the purser called from the

door to the "ballroom." That was what the ship's company insisted on calling the spacious white-walled room, although since New Orleans Justice had seen it used for nothing but the passionate running poker game the purser now called him to.

Ruff nodded, turned wistfully once more toward the silent river, and then strode toward the glare and tumult of the cardroom. He entered, hung his hat on the hook near the door, smoothed back his hair, and walked to the table.

The faces were the familiar ones. Updike, who was rotund and heavy-handed with cards and people; the narrow, bland-eyed George Birch; the cattle buyer from Kansas, Jim Haas; and the woman.

She was the one who held Justice's glance and returned it with clear interest. Her name was Sarah Kent, and she was a tall, blue-eyed woman with a classic figure and a fine skull. She had the look of an aristocrat; her accent was pure Virginia.

"Mr. Justice," she greeted him, and he nodded, sitting as Haas broke open a deck of cards. Updike leaned back in his chair and trimmed a new cigar. Birch's emotionless glance shuttled to Ruff's eyes, held for a moment, and then flitted away.

"Jacks or better, eagle ante," Haas said, and Ruff turned his attention to the table, where neat, bright stacks of gold coins sat against the blue velvet. Smoke drifted into the air in lazy, flat spirals and the cabin boy passed by with a tray of sandwiches and liquor.

Haas riffled the cards and dealt around. Justice arranged his hand, stayed as Birch opened, and kept the two eights Haas had given him.

Sarah kept three cards, found time for a brief cheerful smile in Ruff's direction, and sipped at her sauterne. "You do know that Colorado country, don't you, Mr. Justice?" she asked.

"Yes. I've seen it a time or two," he assured her.

2

"I thought you were from Dakota," Birch said without looking up from his cards.

"I've been there too," Ruff said mildly.

"Mr. Justice has roamed the West," Sarah said effusively. "Why, last evening he was telling me—"

"You going to bet?" Updike asked with a sigh. The fat man shifted heavily in his chair. Poker was a business with him, and he was impatient with this card-party chatter.

"Twenty," Sarah said casually.

Ruff dropped his cards onto the table. He had drawn nothing to go with the eights, and Birch, having opened, obviously had a pair of jacks or better.

"If you're still of the same mind, Sarah," Justice said, "we can talk it over again this evening."

"Oh, yes," she said, frowning briefly over her cards as she stayed with Birch and Updike for another twenty dollars. "After all, I need someone to guide me, don't I?"

"You'd do better to hire someone in St. Jo," Birch grumbled. He looked again at Justice, taking in the long hair, the narrow features of the man, the ruffled shirt. "What do you know about this man?"

"What would I know about a guide from St. Jo?" Sarah asked logically.

Birch grunted an answer and threw down his cards as Updike revealed his full house. "You're winning a hell of a lot," Birch said, shifting his antipathy to the big man.

"I pay attention to the game," Updike snorted.

Justice lifted an eyebrow and studied George Birch briefly. The man had been tempered by hard weather. His hands were tough and brown. Webs of fine lines were engraved around his eyes. There was tension between Ruff and the man, and Justice wasn't sure if it was because Birch disliked him or because there was something between Birch and Sarah Kent.

They acted as if they had never met before New Orleans, and yet Birch was just a little too familiar at times,

3

a little too blunt. Yet maybe that was the way he was with women.

"Are you in?" Updike asked with irritation, and Justice slid a gold eagle into the pot, nodding.

He drew three fours this time, and stayed in for a heavy opening bet from Haas. The cattle buyer's face was an open book—he was holding something solid. Ruff discarded a ten and a five, got another five and a red queen in exchange, and stayed in for one more round of betting. He was aware of Sarah's deep-blue eyes on him, subtly aware of the soft signals she was sending out. He had the idea Birch was aware of them as well. The man's eyes had gone colder yet.

"Fifty more," Haas said, raising again, and Ruff folded. The telltale gleam in the cattle buyer's eyes was brighter than three fours.

Updike stayed with him. Birch folded.

"If you'll stop by my cabin after a while, Mr. Justice," Sarah was saying, "we can make the arrangements. I'll need to know what your salary will be and what provisions to purchase."

"I'll stop in," he said, "and we'll go over it in detail."

"Three aces," Haas said.

"Four deuces," Updike countered, raking in the coins with his thick white hands. Haas was beginning to sweat, and Ruff wondered if he had been playing with money meant to buy cattle.

Updike shuffled and dealt. Ruff got a trash hand. Ten high, a seven, a trey, a jack, and a five. "I'm out," he said as Haas opened—tentatively this time. The hand wasn't worth drawing to.

"Around eight?" Sarah asked. Her eyes were misted, glittering with the candlelight. He nodded his answer. She was intriguing, this woman, and if she was who General Hightower said she was, she was also dangerous.

Birch glowered at him like a jealous lover who has just

been cut out. Haas was pale, his hands trembling just slightly. Ruff felt sure that Haas could afford to lose no more.

"How many?" Updike snapped.

"Two," Haas replied. Birch also took two. Sarah folded, and Updike took three.

But it was the way that he took them that caused Justice's eyes to narrow.

Hadn't that last card come off the bottom? Justice wasn't sure. Justice had sat in on a few card games—he preferred monte—but it wasn't a passion with him, and he would have been the first to admit he wasn't the most skilled at cards. Yet that movement, almost completely shielded by Updike's huge, soft hands, had seemed to be a bottom deal.

Haas lost another thirty. Birch ordered another whiskey, and Updike dealt again. Justice drew two tens and stayed with it, discarding a seven, a black nine, and a six.

Haas opened, almost fearfully, and Birch folded. Ruff kept his eyes on Updike's hands, still not sure. He drew another ten and stayed with the raise, watching the confidence grow on Haas's face. Someone should tell the man he wasn't a poker player.

"What've you got?" Updike asked blandly, and Ruff showed them the tens. Haas's face fell, and Updike pursed his lips.

"Sorry," the fat man said. He spread out four sevens.

Birch yawned; Haas mopped his forehead. Sarah smiled —and Ruff Justice moved.

Updike had his hand on the gold eagles when Ruff's hand shot out and covered the big man's. Updike's eyes went suddenly hard, and the facial muscles beneath the flaccid flesh tightened.

"What the hell are you doing?"

"Give it to Haas," Ruff said. His voice was soft but cold. Updike's eyes flickered.

"What is this, a joke?" Updike asked. His laugh wasn't convincing. Ruff's hand still rested on the fat man's. When Updike tried to pull his hand away, Ruff's tightened on his wrist like a band of iron.

"It's no joke," Justice said, his face intent. "You cheated the man. Give him his money."

"By God, sir, you'll not make unfounded accusations like that!" The purser, his face lined with concern, was inching toward the table. "I've been running card games on this boat for three years!"

"Then likely you've been cheating for three years," Ruff said coldly.

"What in hell is this about, Justice?" George Birch demanded.

"This." Ruff spread out Updike's hand again. "Four sevens."

"Yes?" Birch asked impatiently. "So what?"

Ruff released Updike and turned over his own discards, revealing a fifth seven. "He got a little sloppy," Ruff said. "I guess we're comparatively easy marks."

"Damn your eyes!" Haas sputtered.

Justice looked again at Updike, expecting to see discomfort, embarrassment, anything but what he did see. The man's mask had dropped away. He was no longer an amiable, slightly excitable fat man.

His small mouth had formed into a straight line, his lips compressed until they were white, bloodless. His jaw twitched with unspoken hatred, his small eyes were glowing coals. His expression was pure animal savagery, scarcely under control. If they had been alone in that room then, Justice had no doubt, the man would have lunged at him, trying to tear his throat out, to maim and blind like a wild, vengeful thing. It was pure hatred Updike radiated, and it prickled the back of Ruff's neck. The closest he had come to a look like that was on a moonlit night in New Mexico, up in the Jicarilla Moun-

6

tains, when he had unexpectedly met a cougar on a high narrow trail.

"Mr. Updike," the purser said sternly, "I believe we should have a talk with the captain."

Updike nodded and stood, but his eyes hadn't left those of Justice. His voice when he spoke was a dry hiss. "I'll kill you for this, you bastard. I'll kill you if it's the last thing I do."

He was led away by the purser, Haas tagging behind them after a brief, mumbled thank you to Ruff. Birch was contemplating his whiskey.

"He meant that," Birch said finally. "You've taken away the man's livelihood."

"He'll get over it," Ruff said for Sarah's benefit. Her eyes were shadowed with concern. "Card cheats expect to get caught from time to time."

Birch just shook his head, turning the whiskey glass in his hands. Justice rose and patted Sarah's hand. "It's nothing for you to worry about," Ruff told her. "I'll see you at eight. Your cabin."

She nodded, and Ruff turned toward the door. She seemed reassured, but Ruff was not. The man meant business, and he had let Justice glimpse, just for a minute, the terrible savagery that lay beneath his disarming surface. Ruff swept back his hair and planted his wide-brimmed white hat on his head.

"It was a damned-fool time to get involved in anything," he told himself as he strolled toward his own cabin. He had worked this all very nicely, casually meeting Sarah Kent, slowly gaining her confidence. And what if Updike had calmly pulled a gun and shot him? That would have upset General Hightower's plan neatly.

He shrugged thought of Updike away. Mostly likely the man was now resting in the boat's brig—if it had one—and in the morning he would be behind bars in St. Joseph. Ruff fished for the key to his cabin and went cautiously in. Nothing had been disturbed.

7

He locked the door behind him, pulled off his coat, and stretched out on the comfortable bed, which was covered with a pale-green spread. He gazed at the ceiling and from time to time at the small brass clock beside his bed, listening to the muffled river sounds.

An hour later he rose and stood examining himself in the mirror. He had just decided on a fresh shave when insistent knocking at the door swiveled his head. Frowning, he drew the Colt from his holster and held it beside his leg as he answered the door. It was the purser, Mr. Goodbody.

"Thank God you're all right."

"Why? What's happened?"

"He got away. Mr. Updike. Clean away."

"How in . . . !" Ruff snapped his jaw shut and shook his head. "Let me know when you've got him, will you?"

"Certainly. The captain thinks he jumped over the side, though. He broke away and there was a splash . . ."

"Let me know," Ruff repeated.

"Yes, sir. Sorry, sir."

Ruff nodded, locked the door behind the excited purser, and holstered his pistol. Ruff glanced again at the clock, decided to forget the shave, and pulled on his coat. Updike or no Updike, he wasn't going to miss his appointment with Sarah Kent. Still, he didn't like the idea of the man's lurking out there in the dark.

That business about going over the side was a little shaky. After breaking away from the purser, Updike had only to throw some heavy object overboard and conceal himself. It would be no problem at all, and if he fooled them he could ride on in to St. Jo instead of swimming.

The only way to play it was to figure Updike was on board still and looking for Justice. Updike could have all he wanted, Ruff decided—after he talked to Sarah Kent. That was of prime importance. A lot depended on it.

There were still ten minutes until eight o'clock, but

Ruff was developing cabin fever. Straightening and forming his hat, he turned and went out, locking the door carefully behind him.

From far forward the sounds of voices drifted. The dining room for first-class passengers was that way. A boatman armed with a rifle walked past Ruff, who asked him, "Didn't find him yet?"

"Nah. But we will if he's aboard."

Ruff nodded and strode forward as the big paddlewheeler rolled on, splashing its stolid way up the wide Missouri, the paddles creaking as they clawed through the black water, the steam from the twin stacks above wisping into the dark sky.

Justice was next to the mate's cabin, aft of the engine room, when the shadow moving too quickly, too silently, leaped from the shelter of the projecting boiler shield.

A shoulder barreled into Ruff's chest, and a looping fist caught him flush on the jaw. Slammed back against the railing, he pawed for his Colt, had it wrenched savagely from his hand, and felt a fist drive into his ribs, knocking the breath from him.

Ruff fought back wildly, bringing up a knee which glanced off his attacker's thigh and driving a hard right into the dark blur of his face, feeling the satisfying crunch of gristle being compacted.

But it wasn't enough. A hand arced overhead, and there was something dark, hard, and ominous clenched in it. It landed solidly over Ruff's ear, lighting the interior of his skull with colored stars and a brief, intense sheet of flame.

Then he felt his legs buckle, felt the sickness rising in his stomach. He tried to strike out, but his arms were leaden, agonizingly slow. Hands were locked around Ruff's throat, strangling, iron-fingered hands, the thumbs digging into the jugular. Ruff felt consciousness leaking away, and for a moment he let it take him.

Then his thoughts cleared starkly. He realized fully what was happening, recognized the situation for what it was. This man was killing him!

He was damned if he'd go out that way, not after a life of fighting the Sioux and Cheyenne, of warring with the Apaches. Determination brought desperate strength. Ruff clenched his fists and brought his arms up savagely, inside of his attacker's arms. The hands were torn away from around his throat, and Ruff, choking and gasping, struck out with three fierce right-hand blows. One of them landed solidly on an ear, and the man staggered backward.

But Ruff hadn't the strength to finish it, and before he could set himself he saw the truncheon again lash out, felt it impact with his skull, and a moment later felt the shove of two fisted hands against his chest; he fell backward over the rail and tumbled into the dark river beneath him.

He narrowly avoided the slashing paddles of the riverboat, but the shock as he met the water was nearly as bad. He had fallen from a height, and it was like falling against cement. The breath was driven from him, and he had to fight through a dark web of clinging unconsciousness to force himself to the surface, where he sucked in a long, saving breath of air.

His head still rang, and he had to make an effort to stay conscious. His eyes refused to focus, and the river was cold, deathly cold. His heart thumped heavily in his chest. The riverboat, he knew by the diminishing sound, was far upstream. By willing his vision to clear he finally made out its vaguely white bulk pulling away from him, disappearing around a bend in the Missouri.

Ruff tried to swim and was making a bad job of it before his befuddled brain cleared enough for him to realize he had to shed his waterlogged clothes if he hoped to make it to the shore, which seemed incredibly distant.

The boots, new in New Orleans, were difficult, but he

managed to get them off, letting them sink to the river bottom. He shed his pants and coat more easily, treading water all the while.

The blows to the head had knocked the stamina from Justice's body. That, combined with the cold current, made each swimming stroke an effort. His head was alive with pinpricks of red and yellow light, his chest was on fire. The river was dark, the night black. A few stars sparkled in the cloudy, moonless sky.

The current was swift, and already Ruff knew he was miles from where he had been dumped overboard. He had been swimming for a good half hour, and the dark, formless line of the riverbank seemed as distant as ever.

He rolled onto his back and swam that way for a time, taking it slowly. It was too easy to cramp up in cold water, and there was no rush now anyway. The object was only to survive long enough to crawl ashore, to rest, to sleep.

It was another interminable period before he could do just that.

He reached the bank at a spot where the rushes grew in tangled profusion and the footing was sloppy. He staggered through the reeds and cattails, fighting for each step. The mud sucked at his feet, wanting to draw him back into the river's dark clutches.

Finally he made it. Huge dark oaks loomed overhead, and Ruff dragged himself, cold, slimy, exhausted, onto the dry, grassy bank.

He lay still against the earth, his chest hammering, his breath coming in labored gasps, his teeth chattering with the cold. After a minute he managed to drag himself farther from the water's edge, and, raking up a pile of oak leaves, he burrowed into them, covering himself with this damp and ineffective blanket against the bitter cold of the night.

He stared at the trees towering overhead for a long while, and at the stars that glittered through the gaps in the foliage, and then, mercifully, he fell asleep. A deep, dreamless sleep which lasted until the first harsh red light of dawning, when he was prodded awake with a boot toe which belonged to the grim man with the shotgun in his hands.

# 2.

❖

Ruff squinted into the glare of dawning and sat up. "Mornin'," he said and nodded.

There was still no smile on the big man's rugged face, and the twin muzzles of his scattergun, looking as big as blue iron tunnels, never wavered.

"Who the hell are you?" the big man demanded.

"Ruffin T. Justice is the name," he said, starting to rise.

"Set," the big man said. Ruff sat. "Are you nekked or what?"

"Just about," Ruff had to admit. He brushed a few of the leaves aside, and the big man tilted his head thoughtfully.

"Well, you obviously ain't armed," he said, lowering his shotgun. "I guess you ain't what I thought you was. But you acted almighty funny last night."

"I felt almighty funny."

"Crawlin' up here, sneakin' through the reeds, hidin' under the leaves like that."

"I fell off a riverboat."

"Do tell." The man nodded. "I seen that one pass last evening. Junior!" he yelled, turning his head toward the trees behind him. "Come on out now, it's all right."

Junior came out. A narrow, gangly kid with ears that stuck out like jug handles and no chin at all. His hair was cropped close to his skull, and it was obvious from the dim light in his eyes that Junior was only half at home.

He sidled toward Justice, grinning stupidly and then reverting to apprehension. He stepped behind the big man, peering out at Justice, who had gotten to his feet, dusting the leaves from himself.

"Who did you think I was?" Ruff asked.

"Ah, flatboat pirates. River rats, you know." He jabbed an angry elbow at Junior, who was clinging to him. "They jumped me last time upriver, got six hundred gallons of molasses. We're tied up right the other side of these trees"— he pointed—"and Junior here heard you comin'." Junior grinned.

"I wish I'd known last night," Justice said, trying to stretch some of the kinks out. "I could have done with a blanket or some hot coffee."

"Just as well you didn't try to come over. I likely would have shot you," he said, closing one eye in a heavy wink. "The name's Charley Moore." He thrust out a meaty hand, and Justice took it. "Headin' for St. Jo?"

"I was."

"Throwed you off, did they?"

"I didn't say that."

"You don't look the kind to fall, mister. If you did, you fell hard, judging from that fine collection of knots and bruises you got."

Justice smiled. "I was thrown." He asked Moore, "Any chance of going upriver with you?"

"You ever poled a flatboat?" Moore asked dryly.

"No."

"Well, you're welcome to come with us, but it might be you'd rather walk. It's a labor, son, gettin' them boats upriver."

"I'll work my way," Ruff told him, and Moore nodded, sucking at his lower lip.

"All right. Don't say I didn't warn you." Junior was

peeking over Moore's shoulder, his eyes bright, over-bright.

"It's your hair that's fascinatin' him so," Moore said. "His ma keeps his shaved off because of the ticks and and scabies. Act right, Junior; you seen men with long hair before." He cuffed the boy, but good-naturedly. "He ain't much, is he?"

"He seems friendly, happy." They walked back through the trees to where Moore's laden flatboat was tied back among the heavy brush.

"Oh, yes, he's that. But the lad's dim, powerful dim. He can pole, though! Lord God, he can pole. He'll work till he drops if I don't stop him. He's a good worker."

"That's important," Ruff said, seeing that it made Moore happy.

"Yes, sir," he said proudly. "He does work." With a self-satisfied chuckle Moore leaped from the bank to the waiting flatboat, watching as Justice, dressed only in his shirt, followed. "Junior, find the man somethin' to wear, for God's sake."

The flatboat, Ruff noticed as Moore cast off, was again carrying molasses. Moore read the question in Justice's eyes and explained, "Sumbitches want it to make liquor out of."

He was talking around the stem of a cob pipe which he had stoked up after casting off. Now the riverman stood hunched across the tiller, letting the current drift the flat-boat out of this hidden, shadowed cove.

Once onto the Missouri the work began. Moore kept the flatboat in close to shore, where the current was weaker but still strong enough to drift them back toward the Mississippi.

Junior already had his long pole out, and he was walking the raft. Starting at the bow of the flatboat, he planted his pole in the muddy bottom and walked to the stern, propelling the boat forward with painful slowness.

"We'll pick up a mule-haul near Stanford," Moore told Ruff. "But for now, this is the only way to get upriver."

Ruff, after having been given some coffee and bread, and dressed now in a shabby pair of homespun pants, torn shirt, and battered straw hat, got down a second pole, and following Junior's lead he walked the deck of the flatboat, poling the boat upriver.

The clothes Moore had given him—"Always keep spares; ain't made a trip yet without going over at least once"—itched, and Ruff had the uneasy feeling that there were tiny living stowaways in the homespuns. The sun was hot, the glare off the water brilliant. Mosquitoes plagued them until Moore lit a smudge pot kept for that purpose.

By noon Ruff's shoulders were aching. They had nearly been swamped by a sternwheeler which hooted its whistle derisively as Moore stood shaking his fist, but there was no sign of the molasses pirates.

They made Stanford in the late afternoon, and there lines were secured to the riverboat and tied to the harness of a plodding mule team which walked the riverbank, stolidly towing the boat upriver. Only then did Moore stop to eat.

It was only molasses and bread, but it was filling. Justice perched on the roof of the low cabin, Junior beside him, and, chewing thoughtfully, watched the mules at their unhurried pace plod through the shade of the giant maple and oak trees as sundown colored the western skies and a flight of ducks, flying low across the wide Missouri, headed for the marshes.

It was three slow days to St. Joseph, Missouri. Darkness had already settled when Moore tied up at the wharf alongside a hundred other flatboats. Beyond the wharves the haze of light against the sky marked the city of St. Jo, the jumping-off point for argonauts, fur traders, settlers, and the big wagon trains.

"Thanks, Mr. Moore," Ruff said. "You too, Junior."

Moore shook hands, and Junior offered his own hand tentatively. "You keep on working like you're doing," Ruff said, rubbing the kid's burr head. Junior grinned, and Ruff climbed up a river-damp, gray ladder to the wharf above.

Stopping once to look back and wave, he strode down the long wharf, a barefooted man in outsized pants, his pockets empty and a long, long road ahead of him.

Common sense told him that he had muffed this job and he might as well just pull out. He had foolishly gotten himself tangled up with a petty gambler, been thrown overboard, and probably lost Sarah Kent for good. She was three days ahead of him, and it was unlikely she would have waited in St. Jo on the off chance that her guide might show up eventually.

The general would not be happy about this. Ruff could recall all too vividly the determination on General Hightower's face when he had been called into his office back at Fort Towson in the Indian Nation.

"You're Justice?" the officer had said, making it half question, half statement as he looked up from behind his efficiently arranged desk. A tall, silver-haired man with a soldier's black eyes, he had looked Ruff over without comment. "Sit," he said finally, and Ruff took a seat, crossing his legs, placing his hat on his knee.

Hightower stood and walked around his desk to face Ruff. "General Taylor says you're good."

"He's a friend from way back," Ruff replied.

"Unconventional, I believe he said. But good. Do you know why you're here?"

"No, sir. I was only told it was important."

"You're damned right it is," Hightower said with some emotion. "To me at least." The general had walked to the window, and he stood there now, hands behind his back, watching the heavy rain wash down from the tumultuous skies, silvering his window. "You ever make a mistake, Justice?"

"Too many to count."

"I made a mistake in judgment. It was a mistake which led to a tragedy. I trusted a man, the wrong man, to do a job."

"It happens," Ruff said mildly.

Hightower turned, his eyes sparking. He looked at the lean, long-haired man in buckskins and he nodded agreement. "It happens, but my mistake led to blood." Hightower got down to telling him about it.

"Captain James R. Kent. A bright young officer, combat-tested, Point man. Neat, courteous, handled men and horses with a soft, knowing hand. He was my friend, Justice. As much as a junior officer can be a friend to a man in my position."

Ruff nodded. Hightower perched on the corner of his desk, running a hand across his gray hair. Justice waited patiently for him to continue. The rain drummed down. A cool breeze found its way through the chinked log walls.

"He was our pay officer, you see. I sent Captain Kent to Fort Smith to collect our monthly pay—it was a routine job, he'd done it a dozen times—"

"Captain Kent didn't come back this time," Ruff guessed.

Hightower's eyes narrowed, and he nodded, slapping his hands on his thighs. "That's it. He had four men with him. A second lieutenant, Charles Boggs, three months out of the Point. An old-line NCO, Master Sergeant Kyle, and two enlisted men, Privates Geer and Jefferson."

"They didn't come back either?"

"No." Hightower shook his head. "They couldn't. They were found dead. Executed. The four of them in a row, hands tied behind their backs, shot in the back of the head."

Ruff was silent. Hightower's face was controlled, but his voice had begun to quaver with raw emotion. "I want that man, Justice. I want him badly."

"You've looked for him?"

18

"Of course. But the leads are few. We haven't been able to turn him. The problem, of course," Hightower said, "is that army men tend to look like army men. They get nowhere with a job like this."

"I don't look army," Justice said with some amusement.

"Not very much. But you are a good scout. I know you've had some experience with work like this. I hear you're tough. You're the man I want for this job, Justice. I've combed our files looking for a man like you."

"Where is he?" Ruff asked point-blank.

"Texas? Montana? Paris?" Hightower shrugged heavily. "Who knows? But there is one lead, and an important one. Kent has a sister, his only living relative. She lives in Virginia. Lynchburg, I believe. Or she did live there. She's sold the family house, packed up her belongings, and booked passage on a ship from Baltimore to New Orleans."

"You think it ties in?"

"I do. She's meeting him somewhere. I'd bank on it."

"It's a thin lead, sir," Justice commented.

"It's the only one we've got!" Hightower said, banging his fist against his desk. He wanted this man, all right. Wanted him desperately. It was written on his face, in those dark, hard eyes. "I want you to meet this woman in New Orleans. Somehow, some way, find out where she is going and follow her."

And he had. Riding upriver with Sarah Kent, he had fallen into shipboard conversations with her. The woman was either the coolest liar Ruff had ever met or she was unaware of her brother's crime. She was going to Colorado, she had told him, to live with her family—she had never mentioned Kent by name; perhaps he had told her not to.

"Colorado?" Ruff had smiled to himself as they stood at the rail, the soft breeze in their faces. "Funny, isn't it? That's where I'm heading."

19

"Is it really?" she had asked with pleased astonishment. "I'm worried about the trip—the Indians and all. I wish there was someone I knew, someone who could take me through to Colorado."

Ruff had graciously volunteered. All that was left to do was to make the final arrangements, acquire provisions; and then all of the planning had been toppled by a moment's irritation at a cheap gambler.

Sarah had never said definitely where she was going—maybe her brother had cautioned her about that as well. Colorado. Somewhere in Colorado, somewhere within a hundred thousand square miles. The smart thing to do would be to pull off the job now, but he could visualize Hightower's face as he read the wire. It was going to be hard enough to telegraph for more funds—everything Ruff had in the way of money was at the bottom of the Missouri River.

There was still a light in the office of the steamship company, and Ruff went in. Heads turned toward him. A tall, lean man in baggy homespun pants, bare feet sticking out below the cuffs.

"Yes?" The clerk behind the desk nearly lurched to his feet, gawking.

"Ruffin T. Justice is the name. I was hoping you might have a trunk that belongs to me."

"Mr. Justice! Yes. The captain reported that you fell overboard. A terrible thing. Terrible. I hope you don't hold the company to blame—"

"Could I have my trunk, please?" The little man nodded three times.

"Of course."

The clerk scurried off toward the back of the office. Two prim, older ladies backed away from Justice as he followed the clerk. They entered a back room which had wire on the windows, and Ruff spotted his blue trunk in the corner. The clerk watched in apprehension as Justice took a fire ax from the wall and smashed the hasp open.

"Lost the key," Ruff explained with a smile.

"Are you sure you're . . . ?" He looked again at the tall ragged man before him.

"I am. These clothes will fit. Mind if I dress here?"

"No, of course not, but . . ."

"Thanks." Ruff dropped his trousers and stripped off his shirt while the clerk leaped for and closed the storeroom door.

Ruff found his buckskin pants, stepped into them, and asked the clerk, "Did they catch Updike?"

"Who? Oh, the gambler. I don't believe so," the little man answered, wagging his head.

The clerk seemed fascinated by Ruff's clothes. Buckskin pants and shirt, bleached white, with Indian beadwork and long fringes. His boots were similarly fringed, and the hat Ruff removed from the trunk was broad, flat-brimmed, and decorated with a red plume. There was also a gunbelt from which a long-barreled Colt dangled, and at the back of the belt a Bowie with a murderously long blade. A small ivory-handled skinning knife was taken from the trunk and slipped into a scabbard which was stitched to the side of Ruff's boot.

There was nothing else in the trunk but shaving gear, soap, a towel, and two small black books. As the clerk watched, Ruff picked up the rest of his belongings and prepared to leave.

"Have you got some kind of a sack?" Ruff asked.

"Yes, surely." The clerk led the way back into the now deserted office and, fishing under the counter, came up with a small cotton sack. "First Bank of Missouri" was stenciled on the side.

"Will this do?"

"It will." Ruff placed the books and toilet articles inside, touched his hat brim, and turned toward the door, the clerk staring after him for a long minute before he returned to his work.

St. Jo was booming. Bustling crowds filled the broad

21

dusty streets. Ox teams hitched to ponderous Conestogas lowed incessantly. From the saloons there was a clamor of hectic sound. People from all corners of the nation walked the streets. Settlers with their long, stoic faces, sunbonneted wives clinging to their arms, Texas cowboys, dark-suited businessmen, sailors, and narrow-eyed sharpers.

Ruff strode among them, angling toward the nearest hotel, the sack slung over his shoulder. Sarah, if she was still here, would be difficult to find in this wildly crowded town. It was much more likely that she had traveled on by now, however, and if finding her in St. Jo. was difficult, finding her trail on the plains was even more improbable. But there was little to do but press on.

Justice tramped into the hotel and placed his sack on the counter, waiting until the narrow-faced, spectacled clerk was finished with another customer.

"Yes, sir," the clerk greeted Ruff. "Please sign the book. Two dollars in advance."

"I'll pay when I leave," Justice said. The clerk's smile washed away.

"But it is required that you pay in advance, sir." He glanced uneasily at Justice's luggage—a small cotton sack. "Otherwise," the clerk said with a shake of his head, "we can't—"

Help came from an unexpected quarter. Two dollars were slipped onto the counter, and Ruff turned to find Haas beside him, looking prosperous and relaxed.

"I appreciate that," Ruff said. "I'll pay you back."

"Nonsense. If it hadn't been for you I'd be flat broke, and you know it. I'm ashamed to admit it, but that wasn't even my money I was gambling with," the cattle buyer said unnecessarily. "It's a shame that Updike got away, though."

"You haven't seen him in St. Jo?" Ruff asked.

"No, but I don't doubt he's here. If I see him . . ." Haas let the threat drop. It was a threat he couldn't back

22

up anyway, and both he and Justice knew it. He stood for a moment looking into the cold blue eyes of a man who he knew instinctively could back up any threat he made, and he nodded, tentatively touching Ruff's shoulder.

"If you need any more money, just ask."

"Hold it. Does this price include meals?" Ruff asked the clerk.

"No, sir. At one time—"

"Lend me another five and I'll see it's well spent," Justice said, interrupting the hotel man. Haas did so without hesitation.

"If you want a hundred, just say so."

"I just might," Ruff said, and Haas's face fell a little, as if he had made an impulsive error.

"Well," Haas said, looking around, "I've some people waiting for me. Good luck to you, Justice, and thanks."

Haas walked away a little stiffly and joined three other beefy businessmen. Ruff watched for a moment, accepted the key from the hotel clerk, and climbed the carpeted stairs toward his room.

The room was dark and cool. The curtains had been opened, the window left open to air the room. Justice tossed his sack onto the bed, crossed to the window, and after watching the noisy, crowded street for a minute, he closed it.

He lighted the cheap coal-oil lamp in the corner and sagged into the only chair, hearing it squeak beneath him as the joints separated a little more.

He would have to wire General Hightower for funds, and he hated that, but there was no other way. While waiting he would have to scour the town, find out if Sarah was by some chance still in St. Jo, and if not, try to discover which way she had gone. She must have hired a guide or perhaps hooked on with a wagon train, so maybe someone would recall. In the meantime there was nothing to do.

He was hungry, tired, and dirty. It was a toss-up which

23

of these matters should be taken care of first, but his stomach finally won out.

Snatching up his hat, Ruff walked to the door and went out. He frowned, and his hand dropped to his belted gun. The corridor was empty. Now. But for just a fragment of a second he had seen a shadowy figure at the end of the hall, seen the quick withdrawal as he came out of his door.

Updike? It was possible, all too possible; he recalled the man's vivid anger, the oath. *If it's the last thing I do,* he had said, *I'll kill you.* And Justice had believed him, damned if he hadn't.

The problem was, of course, that Updike wouldn't have to see to it personally. Men could be hired for ten dollars drinking money to chop up a stranger in an alley. Each face Ruff saw would become suspect. A bootblack, a river rat, an idle cowboy. Every man in St. Jo was a potential assassin, and Ruff found himself suddenly not liking the city at all.

He knew St. Jo reasonably well. He had swung through it with Bill Cody's Wild West Show years back, the only time that Hickok had traveled with them, and by God hadn't that been a time! Hickok shooting out every candle in the Longhorn Saloon one by one, Cody applauding at each shot, leading the saloon crowd in a cheer. Jesus, it would be a long time before Ruff forgot that trip, and it could never happen again, not now. That bastard Jack McCall had murdered Hickok, and Cody, tired of the real thing, had taken up a Barnum-like career of reliving past glories endlessly.

And what's at the end of the line for you, Justice? he thought dispiritedly. A showman, an old man, retelling the past endlessly, or a bullet in the back of the head in some dirty, godless hole?

Justice shook these thoughts aside. They came infrequently, but powerfully. The city seemed to bring them

24

on. The city with its dirt and vermin, blazing lights and hooting voices. Never out there.

Out there where the long winds blew, where nature was savage and raw, where death could be faced honorably. Out there where a man meant something, where a single man could mean the difference . . .

He turned into the Western Union office, scribbled his message to Fort Towson's commanding officer, and paid over three of Haas's dollars.

He ate in a small neat restaurant surrounded by sod-busters who griped at the dollar price for a meal of grits, potatoes, steak, beans, hot bread and honey, coffee, and greens.

The night had quieted some when he came out of the restaurant. The saloons were still howling with noise: tinkling glass, overturned chairs, the occasional screech of a woman, loud laughter, but the rest of St. Jo seemed to have turned in.

Justice walked the silent, dark streets, his boot heels making only a faint click against the new plank walks which decorated this end of St. Jo. The rows of mercantile stores, prime suppliers for the westbound trade, stared out at Justice with blank eyes. Wispy clouds paved the black, late sky.

"Sir?"

Justice slowed his walk. A small, anxious-looking woman in yellow stood at the mouth of an alley, her hands clasping a black reticule tightly.

"What is it?" He stopped and regarded the woman, Young, round-cheeked, a wisp of dark hair curling across her forehead. She held that purse as if her life depended on it.

"There's a man following me." She looked nervously up the street.

"I don't see anyone," Ruff said.

"But I'm sure of it. He knows I've got . . . well, quite

25

a bit of money with me." She hesitated. "Would you, could you possibly escort me back to my hotel? Its the Missouri House," she added, nodding in the direction of the ancient hotel on the river.

Ruff smiled lightly. The girl looked frightened to death. "Of course, miss." He bowed slightly, and she smiled.

"Could you possibly carry my purse?" she asked, and again Ruff nodded amiably.

"Certainly."

She held it out, and he stepped to her, taking the purse from her small, narrow hands. It was then that they jumped him.

Rough hands pawed at him, trying to drag him into the alley, and Ruff kicked out, taking one of the two men square in the groin. He folded up, moaning and writhing, but the second man was on top of Ruff.

Justice saw the silver flash of a knife, and he side-stepped, bringing up his Colt. He slammed it down hard on the man's wrist, hearing the crack of bone. The man went down hard, and Ruff swung back to face the other attacker, who had gotten to his feet, holding his groin in agony.

Ruff raised his Colt, and the man took off on the fly, darting into the black alleyway. Ruff banged a shot after him, heard it strike wood, and lowered his gun. The second man had crawled away, cradling his shattered wrist, and Ruff let him go.

"Well, you were right, it appears," Ruff said, turning, but the girl was gone. Ruff frowned, holstered his pistol, and picked up the woven purse which the girl had left behind.

He opened it and turned it over. Empty. Absolutely empty.

Ruff stepped back out into the street, watching for a moment, seeing no one. Minutes later two men came rushing toward him, summoned by the shot, no doubt, and Ruff turned on his heel, striding away from the alley, wondering if he was beginning to get old and soft.

That had been a neat trap, the girl even giving him the purse to occupy his hands. It would have worked, but the men seemed to be amateurs. A professional would have taken Ruff down with one swift bullet.

So what was it? A clumsy attempt at robbery, or one of Updike's plans gone wrong? He recalled the shadowy figure in the hotel corridor.

There was no telling at this point. Ruff only knew that he was beginning to dislike St. Jo intensely. He slept lightly that night, a chair propped under the door handle in his room, the big Colt revolver in his hand.

# 3.

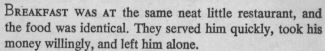

Breakfast was at the same neat little restaurant, and the food was identical. They served him quickly, took his money willingly, and left him alone.

After eating he walked out into the active streets, seeing the sunlight glinting on the distant Missouri, watching the dust at the edge of town from a departing wagon train. The dust could be seen for miles, billowing up strongly, flooding the skies, before slowly dissipating, settling, like a lot of the dreams those sodbusters carried with them would do.

After a quick stop at the telegraph office, Ruff started checking each hotel in St. Jo. The fourth one, the Kensington, repaid his efforts.

"Miss Sarah Kent . . . ? Yes, she was here. One night only." The deskman looked up dreamily. "I recall her because of those soft eyes, that sleek neck. Man, is that a woman. Gentle voice, but a quick smile . . ."

"When did she leave?" Ruff asked. The man could save his daydreaming for later.

"Like I said, she was here one night. Three days back, the fourteenth, she paid and left."

"Alone?"

"I'm not sure, mister." The man's eyes held uncertainty now.

"Look, I'm just a friend," Ruff said reassuringly.

"Well, she might have been alone, but I don't think so. Two men helped her with her luggage—she was carrying considerable luggage."

"What did they look like?"

The man shrugged. "I wasn't really looking at 'em that close."

He had been looking at sleek necks and bouncing bustles, no doubt. Ruff pushed it. "City men? Cowboys, plainsmen, what?"

"Look, mister, I'm not sure . . ." His eyes looked Ruff's buckskins up and down. "I think one of them was wearing dirty buckskins. Maybe he had a beard, I seem to recall one, but I can't swear to it."

"And the other man?"

"I've got no recall of him."

"Do you know where they took the luggage?"

"I sure don't. Look, I'm sorry, friend, but I got work to do, and I can't help you no more. All I remember is the woman." Ruff left the man to his memories.

It was dry outside, hot with the scent of the river but none of its coolness in the air. Ruff began methodically checking the supply houses, never forgetting to glance over his shoulder, to stay away from the shadowed alleys. Someone in St. Jo wanted his hide; they couldn't have it just yet.

The huge, busy storekeeper in bib overalls was loading hundred-pound sacks of flour onto a settler's cart. He was grouchy with the heat, but when Ruff bent to lend him a hand, he answered his questions.

"I recall her," the storekeeper said. He grunted, hefting another sack. "Beautiful woman. She came in with Wade Kesselring. Stocked up a wagon, paid gold money. Colorado, I believe she said."

"Kesselring say which way he was going?"

"Not outright." The big man stopped to mop his profusely perspiring brow. "But I heard him say somethin' about Fort Riley if they needed to exchange horses."

Ruff thanked him and walked back toward the Western Union office, his spirits rising. Kesselring was a good man, a known quantity. Ruff had hunted with him up along the Platte one spring. The woman was in good hands, at least.

They were headed for Fort Riley on the Kansas River, towing a heavily laden wagon. With a little luck and no Kiowas, Ruff thought he could beat them to Riley. He tramped into the Western Union office and waited while the clerk found the yellow envelope from General Hightower.

The note was terse, humorless, but Justice was authorized to draw two hundred dollars from the First Missouri Bank.

With gold in his pockets, he purchased a new Henry repeater, a hundred rounds of ammunition, and his food supplies. At the second stable he went to he found what he wanted—a five-year-old chestnut gelding with strong bones and a deep chest, sound as a dollar, as he found out after running it around the block. The chestnut was hardly breathing hard when he reined up.

"That's a damned fine horse, mister," the stableman assured him. "Picked him up from a gambler who needed a stake—or get-out money, he never did say which."

"How about a pack mule? Got anything worth buying?"

The stableman looked offended. "Mister, this is Missouri," he said, stretching the name out, "there ain't no place else to find a decent mule."

The mule he showed him was a fine-looking animal, two hands taller than the chestnut, with a white muzzle, good conformation, and heavily muscled haunches. The animal was surprisingly tame.

"Just don't get him riled," Ruff was advised. "I bought this'n off a man with a milk cart. Mule didn't want to go and the man took a stick to him. Kicked that milk cart to kindling, he did."

By noon Ruff had checked out of the hotel, packed the

mule, and headed west, leaving St. Jo behind. The wind was stirring now, bending the long grass before him. The empty plains, cut across by wagon tracks, stretched out for miles.

He settled into leather, feeling like a man reborn. He loved the empty land and the wild places, the freedom and the shadows of danger. There was nothing like it—just the easy movement of a good horse beneath him, the wind and high skies, the soft whispering of the saddle leather. He relaxed completely, not pushing the horse, which had been stabled up for a long while and was likely out of shape.

He relaxed, liking the day, the wild country, the freedom—but from time to time he turned in the saddle, looking down the backtrail. There was a killing man back in St. Jo, and maybe he too thought it was time to be riding on.

Ruff camped that night on a low knoll where a dead, gray cottonwood tilted against the sky. He lit no fire. In St. Jo there was Kiowa talk. A wagon train had been hit three weeks earlier. He lay beneath the starry skies, watching the night wheel past behind the wrought iron of the dead trees' limbs, and after a time he slept.

He awoke with a start at midnight. He clawed for his Colt, sitting upright slowly. The night was still, the plains seemed empty. But something had nudged a subconscious nerve and brought him out of his dead sleep. What?

The chestnut was cropping grass, the sounds clear in the stillness. The mule looked at him with wide white eyes. Its ears were folded back warily.

Ruff heard nothing, saw nothing, but he stayed awake the rest of the night. He broke camp at sunrise, heading westward with the sun.

He lifted the chestnut into a canter, and the miles flowed past. The horse was obliging, long-winded, and by alternately walking and running it he made good time and kept it reasonably fresh.

He crossed the Kansas River on the next day, seeing the dark, square bulk of Fort Riley rising slowly from the flat plains surrounding it as he drew nearer.

It was late afternoon, the shadows creeping out from the stockade walls, when Ruff made the fort. Stepping down, he loosened the cinches on the chestnut and mule, dusted off, and walked across the parade ground past a formation of men toward the sutler's store. A covered wagon was tied up in front of the store, and Ruff paused, stroking the muzzle of one of the oxen. Walking slowly to the back of the wagon, he lifted the flap and peered in.

There wasn't much to see. Sacks of flour and sugar, a packed trunk—and a woman's skirt hung up to dry.

"Can I help you?" the voice drawled. It was a familiar voice, and Ruff turned slowly, letting the flap down.

"Hello, Birch," Ruff said.

"What are you doing here?" Birch wanted to know. Those flat eyes studied Justice intently.

"Is this Sarah Kent's wagon?"

"You know it is," Birch answered.

"Well, I'm in the right place then. She hired me as guide, remember?"

"We've got another guide. We don't need you."

"*We?* Just what in hell are you doing here, Birch? Kind of attached yourself to the lady?"

"She was alone; she needed somebody," Birch said. The answer was entirely unsatisfactory.

"She has somebody now," Ruff told him.

"I told you, you're not—"

"Mr. Justice!" The voice was warm and enthusiastic. Ruff turned to find Sarah Kent standing on the sutler's boardwalk, a parcel in her hands.

"Miss Kent," Ruff said, removing his plumed hat and bowing low. She smiled in response. Moving to the wagon, she stowed her package away.

"I'm so happy to see you. After you disappeared, why, everyone was afraid you were . . . dead."

"Still kicking, as you can see," Ruff said. "And ready to begin work."

"Oh, dear." Her fingertips went to her lips. "That is a problem. You see, when you didn't show up, we had to hire another man."

The other man appeared just then, ambling through the sutler's door, a growth of mad white whiskers nearly covering his red, round face. A pipe which seemed to threaten those whiskers was poked into a gap which must have been his mouth. He wore dirty buckskins and a dirty and torn flop hat with an eagle feather tucked into the band, and he carried a big Sharps .50 rifle.

"Great God!" he boomed, catching sight of Ruff. "Damn me for a Yankee and stomp me flat if it ain't Mr. Ruffin T. Justice!"

Ruff grinned. "Howdy, Kesselring. Got yourself thatched since I saw you last."

Kesselring touched his beard and grinned—at least, his whiskers rearranged themselves. He stepped from the boardwalk and poked out a huge, weather-dried hand which Ruff took warmly.

"Best damn scout on the high plains, was Mr. Justice," Kesselring said loudly enough to inform every man on the post. "Beat me with a Cheyenne stick! What are you doin' out here, Ruff?"

"Traveling with you, it looks like," Justice answered.

Kesselring's eyes narrowed, then brightened. "Good. We can use another gun, 'specially one like yours. Kiowas are acting fussy."

"I can't see why we need two scouts," George Birch said irritably. "Why pay two men for the job!"

Sarah didn't seem to hear him. She had eased closer to Ruff, and with her head tilted back she was looking at his face with those blue, blue eyes.

"Well, shucks," Ruff said with a faint irony which didn't elude Birch, "you don't have to pay me. Kesselring's got the job. I'm just tagging along. I'm heading for

Colorado too, as I told you. The more the merrier, wouldn't you say, Mr. Birch?"

"Damn sight safer," Kesselring said.

"Why, there's no need to discuss this at all, George," Sarah Kent told him. "Mr. Justice is heading our way. Just as you happened to be going to Colorado."

"Why, Mr. Birch never mentioned that on the boat," Ruff commented.

Birch's eyes flickered with annoyance, but he answered calmly. "It never came up." Birch looked from Justice to Sarah and back again. Then he excused himself quickly. "I've a few more goods to buy."

Sarah watched as the man trudged back into the sutler's store. When the door had closed behind Birch, she turned slowly to Justice and said in a whisper, "I don't know why, but I don't quite trust Mr. Birch."

"You don't have to keep him around then, Sarah. I can run him off, you know."

"Oh, no! I wouldn't want to do that. He really was quite a help to me back in St. Jo and on the trail. No," she said and shook her head, "that wouldn't be right. And I do like Mr. Birch, really. It's just that something's not quite right with him. I didn't think he was planning to go to Colorado until we landed in St. Jo. Then he said he'd help me, since you had disappeared. It's almost as if he were tagging along, following me." She frowned. "But that is ridiculous, isn't it? After all, why would anyone wish to follow me to Colorado?" she asked, and Ruff didn't answer. The only answer he could offer would be one she wouldn't want to hear.

But what about Birch? Who was he? One of James Kent's men sent to escort his sister? Possible. Highly possible, Ruff decided. Sarah offered another possibility. "Perhaps I shouldn't have mentioned the gold mine to Mr. Birch."

"Gold mine?"

"Yes," she said ingenuously. "My . . . family has an

34

interest in a mine in Colorado. That's why we're relocating there. They've already taken a substantial amount of gold from it."

Ruff frowned. So that was Kent's story to his sister. "Come west, Sis, we've hit gold." If Birch was tagging along to try to get in on a hot mining claim, he was following the wrong star. Justice knew exactly where that gold had come from, and it had nothing at all to do with pick-and-shovel work. Mr. Birch was liable to be a very disappointed man. Or a dead one if he tried to horn in on James Kent.

They rolled out of Fort Riley at dawn, the warnings of the camp CO still ringing in their ears. A Kiowa named Bald Horse was running rampant. Six settlers' homes burned, five people dead, an army pack train ambushed. Bald Horse was bad medicine, and the colonel had practically begged them to stay at Riley.

"We're heading into Colorado, colonel," Ruff had told him. "If we wait the snows will start; if it snows we'll never reach Colorado."

The captain seemed upset by the decision. For good reason—he was responsible ultimately for every incident in his jurisdiction. But he didn't order them not to go. Finally, reluctantly, he just gave Justice a short briefing on where and when Bald Horse had last been sighted.

The first day out they passed one of the burned-out farms. The scent of dead smoke was still in the air. No one made a comment about it, but Sarah looked shaken. She had seen only tame Indians in Virginia, and few of those. No one had called Bald Horse tame.

Kesselring led the way, earning his keep as scout, and Ruff had to admit the man knew Kansas better than he did. They didn't want for water or waste time trying to find the right crossing at the coulees. Kesselring knew where he was going and how to get there. He kept them moving.

Birch had been stony silent since Riley, and for a time

Ruff thought the man might turn back. Maybe he had come too far to do that now, maybe the glittering thoughts of a nonexistent gold mine prodded him forward across the long, dry plains.

Night camp was made on the Smoky Hill River, a few miles south of the tiny settlement of Salina.

Birch sat glumly on his saddle drinking coffee while Kesselring added the latest in his long line of Kiowa tales—hair-raising and unsettling to Sarah. Justice gestured him to silence, rose, and stretched.

"I'm going to take a little walk down to the river," Justice said.

"Sarah rose almost too quickly, and Kesselring smiled. "I'd like to go along," she said, and Justice nodded.

"It's not safe," Birch said sourly.

"I'll be safe enough with Mr. Justice," she answered pertly.

"I wouldn't wager on that," Kesselring said so quietly that no one heard him.

"You're welcome to come," Ruff said, and after Sarah got a shawl from the wagon they walked away from the soft red glow of the fire into the still night.

It was clear and cool. Stars glittered against the vast sky, and the oaks along the river swayed in unison to the gentle urging of the night breeze. They walked along the riverbank listening to the chorus of frogs, the chirping of crickets. A silver quarter-moon was drawing itself lazily above the black line of the horizon, and it glossed the dark river.

"It's beautiful out here," Sarah said. "Beautiful, desolate, lonely."

"All of that and more," Ruff answered. He halted near a gnarled oak tree and leaned against a low-growing limb. "But wait until you've seen Colorado, with those high bulking mountains and long green mountain meadows. You'll never want to leave again."

Sarah stepped nearer to him, holding her shawl with

both hands. Her dark hair was free from restraint and flowed down across her back and shoulders. The coming moon sparkled in her eyes.

"I'm so glad you caught up with us, Mr. Justice," she said, and her voice was soft, quite low. "You know, I expected you to come to my cabin that last night on the boat. I wanted to talk about business, but I also thought we might . . . speak personally."

"Maybe that's what got me tossed overboard," Ruff suggested.

"But I thought Mr. Updike did that."

"Well, so did I. But now I'm not so sure. I never did see the man clearly. Just a black, hard-knuckled shadow. I wonder now if maybe Mr. Birch there wasn't jealous. He doesn't want me along, that's for sure."

"But I do." She had taken another step, and her voice had deepened still more. It was a husky, primitive invitation, that voice, and when her head dipped forward, her lips parted in a more definite, urgent invitation.

Ruff kissed her deeply. Her mouth was fluid, aggressive. Her lips were pliant, soft, and stirring. He wrapped his arms around her, and she practically fell against him.

"My knees!" She laughed. "I've never been kissed like that."

He didn't quite believe that, but it didn't matter. Her body was against his in the night, and her breath was close and warm against his cheek.

"They'll miss us if we're gone too long," Sarah whispered.

"You want to head back?"

"I want to hurry!" she replied. Her eyes were laughing, eager, and Ruff, smiling in return, let his fingers trail off her shoulders and go to the buttons down the front of her dress.

She watched with anticipation, with a quickening pulse, as he unbuttoned her and slid the dress off her white shoulders, letting it rustle gently to the ground. She helped him with the ties of her chemise, keeping her lips to his as she worked.

Then she was free of all encumbrance. The moonlight glossed and shadowed her body, making it magically sensual. Her breasts were full, slightly upthrust, with large dark aureoles around the taut, compelling nipples. Ruff bent his lips to her breasts, searching them intimately, pausing at the nipples. Her hands were in his dark hair, and he could hear the thudding of her heart beneath the smooth fullness of her breasts.

"Let's go back here a ways," he suggested, nodding toward the trees which grew tightly along the river, and she collected her clothing in a loose bundle, following him like a lithe wood nymph into the oaks.

Her legs flashed golden in the moonlight. Long, slender, firm, her buttocks full, solid. Ruff led her into a sheltered clearing, and she let her clothes fall from her arms as he moved to her, wrapping his long arms around her, his hands running across her supple back, her smooth, night-cooled hips as she sagged against him, her mouth at his throat, her hands dropping to his crotch, where Ruff's needs were undeniably evident.

"My," she whispered, and there was a tremulous amusement in her voice. Her hand had found his erection beneath the buckskin of his pants, and she measured it for heft and length, not finding him lacking, and he smiled, kissing her temple.

"Still in a hurry?" he asked.

"More than ever. Please do hurry." He stepped back, and her hand remained on his crotch, her eyes sparkling, as he pulled his shirt up and over, sat to remove his boots, and stood again, untying his buckskin pants.

Then she was against him, her crotch warm, fuzzy, grafted to his throbbing erection. Her mouth was hungry, searching, as she kissed him; her breasts were warm, flattened against his chest. "Down," she whispered, "down, down," and he complied.

They made a rough bed of his garments, Ruff going to his back, as Sarah, still clinging to him, followed him closely down.

She slid back, straddling him on her knees. She sat across his legs, her hands running up and down his thighs, her fingers marveling at the conformation of his thigh muscles briefly before creeping to his crotch, where with small excited puffs from her pursed lips she searched his cock from shaft to head.

"My," she said again, "my, that's nice." Her hands trembled, and Ruff noticed her face was deep in sensual concentration. She cupped his sack in her palm, hefting it as Ruff lay with his hands behind his head, gazing up at the stars, at the shadowy outline of this feminine night creature whose hands roamed his body with commanding interest.

The night was soft, and he closed his eyes, feeling the warm contact of her thighs, the soft tracings of her fingers moving along his erection, circling the head of it delicately, the brush of her hair against his thighs as she leaned nearer, studying him by moonlight, clutching the maleness, the strength of him.

Then she could endure it no longer and she scooted forward. Ruff felt the damp brush of her crotch against his thigh, felt her hands against his chest and the slow settling of her heavy, capable hips as she positioned herself across his pelvis.

Her breasts were lazy, full pendulums over him, and as she bent lower, the moonlight in her hair, her nipples just grazed his chest, sending electric impulses through Sarah's body.

Ruff's own body was a seething caldron. His blood collected in his erection, his loins pulsed slowly, deeply. As she bent over him, her dark sleek hair brushing his cheeks and her warm pliant lips meeting his again, he could take no more.

He grabbed her roughly by the hair and pressed his mouth to hers, and she responded with a hard thrust of her pelvis which smeared her body against Ruff's crotch.

His hands dropped to her buttocks, slid across and around their fantastic smoothness, feeling the poised strength there. Dipping down behind her, his fingers found and clung to the sweet stickiness of her body, and she began to tremble.

Her hand looped back and she groped for his cock. Finding it, she gave a small shudder of satisfaction, and, lifting her hips higher as Ruff stroked her to higher levels of need, she positioned him and slowly sank onto his length.

She sat upright, her hands on his abdomen, for a moment, her head thrown back, dark hair cascading across her white, moon-painted shoulders. Her mouth was half open, her eyes half closed in sensual meditation as Ruff filled her, feeling the close, warm contact of her body.

And then, tentatively, she began to move against him as if it were an agony to shift more than a bare inch at a time. Her hips lifted slowly and then slowly settled, Ruff aware of every ridge, button, small clenching of her muscles, of her astounding inner heat.

Slowly she moved, experimentally. She lifted her hips an inch more, her face a study in concentration, and then just as slowly she thrust her pelvis forward. Touching a sensitive, sweet point, she sucked in her breath sharply and her rapt face became almost puzzled.

Ruff let her have her way. She moved searchingly, and now as he watched through drooping eyelids her fingers moved to her own crotch where with wonder and amazement she felt her own eager flesh, and Ruff entering her, thick, satisfying, too pleasurable to be endured.

She stroked herself, clutched at Ruff, and began to sway more intently. Her eyes were washed out behind a veil of need, her face went slack. She lifted her hips and thrust against him, writhed and began to pant with effort. She became fluid inside, and her scent filled the night, flooding Ruff's nostrils as her stroking body began to have its inevitable effect.

She had had her way, but now he couldn't lie there and take it. His own blood was pounding, there was a deep, urgent need building in his loins, and he reached out, taking her by the neck, pulling her against him, kissing her, pressing his lips to hers until her mouth must have hurt, but she made no objection, did not try to pull away. Her tongue slipped inside his mouth, dueled with his tongue, buried itself against his cheek and tried to burrow down his throat as her mouth sucked at his as she ground her breasts against his hard chest, as her hips writhed.

Justice's hands found her hips, and he clenched her buttocks, amazed at the strength there, at the fullness, the easy roll and pitch of them as she thrust against him, as she tried to gobble him, devour him, and he was lost suddenly in a whirling tunnel of sensation, a kaleidoscopic world where there was only sensation, the only object to split the woman in two, to crawl inside of her, to cleave her, to fill her, and he bucked against her, meeting her fury of need with his own hard, nearly savage efforts.

He clawed at her buttocks, dipped low to feel her silky, dewy flesh, to touch his own driving erection, to meet her hand and have their fingers intertwine as they touched first him then her in a mad sensual melee until there was no thought, no function but driving against her, feeling her suck and demand of him, and she burst on top of him, clawing at his shoulders, writhing in orgasm, and Ruff followed her into it, his climax sudden, hard, necessary.

They clung together in the night, their bodies slick with perspiration. Her lips roamed his shoulders, his throat, his face. His hands ran across her back, across the swell of her hips, and she clenched her legs tightly, holding him inside.

He felt her tremble, felt her fingertips on his shoulder, and then, abruptly, the tension, the very life, seemed to go out of her body and she sagged against him, her body fitting itself perfectly to his, each contour melting against his, utterly natural, completely at ease.

Then, amazingly, she slept. Deep in the arms of exhaustion. Ruff smiled and lay still, letting his fingers run along the knuckles of her spine, across the ridges of her wing bone, through the soft screen of her silky hair to the nape of her neck.

The moon glinted through the trees, the stars faded before its light. Far away an owl hooted against the night. Sarah shifted just slightly, her thigh slipping against his, and Ruff yawned.

And then the night exploded with sound, the close guns shattering the stillness, the moment of peace. Ruff rolled the woman aside and dove for his gun, knowing it could already be too late.

# 4.

Ruff rolled from the ground, yanking his Colt from his holster as he came to his feet in the deep shadows. The guns beyond the trees sounded again in loud, heavy staccato. A man bellowed in pain.

Sarah, eyes wide with sleepy terror, crawled toward him, opening her mouth to speak or to scream, and Ruff touched a finger to his lips.

At times like this a man should be dressed, but it wasn't important enough to stop and do it. Naked, he crept through the underbrush, pistol beside his head, thumb on the hammer, Sarah in a crouch behind him.

He saw the first Kiowa before they had the camp in view. A tall, nearly naked brave with his face painted yellow and white, a sawed-off musket in his hands, was crawling forward toward the camp. The moonlight illuminated his bronzed shoulders, outlined him perfectly.

At the sound of Ruff's footsteps he turned and fired in one motion, rolling onto his back. Ruff felt the hot blast from the muzzleloader against his cheek, but the bullet flew wide, tearing the bark off a gnarled black oak beside him.

Sarah screamed, and he could have strangled her for that. Lunging, Ruff collided with the brave, his naked body against the wildly struggling Kiowa. The brave tried for the knife at the back of his belt, but he was too late.

Ruff leaned back, drove his knee hard into the Kiowa's rib cage, and then slammed down the barrel of his Colt. The Indian's struggling ceased instantly and he sagged against the earth, eyes open to the moonlight.

Sarah screamed again, and this time he could have kissed her for it. Tangled up with the man on the ground, he hadn't seen the second Kiowa rushing toward him, hatchet uplifted. Ruff rolled onto his back, propped against the body of the dead Indian, and fired just as the Kiowa dove toward him, hatchet held aloft.

Ruff's Colt bucked in his hand, and he saw the Indian's chest flood with gore. Still, there was no stopping the impetus of his hurtling body, and he collided with Ruff Justice, slamming him to the earth, and Ruff steeled himself for the bite of his hatchet.

But the Kiowa would never move again. He was dead, a fist-sized hole blown open in his chest, his blood streaming out, coating Ruff's chest and belly.

Ruff shook the man off and, racing to Sarah, grabbed her wrist. The camp was still under attack. Intermittently the heavy boom of Kesselring's big buffalo gun could be heard, interspersed with the shots of lighter weapons.

The wagon had been spilled onto its side, whether by Kesselring himself or the attacking Kiowas there was no telling. But Kesselring had positioned himself behind it and was engaged in a fierce firefight with half a dozen Indians.

Sarah was close to Ruff, practically clinging to him as he edged closer. By chance he had come out at a spot where he could see the backs of three of the attackers. It was no time to be squeamish about back-shooting them, and Ruff settled the front sight of his Colt on the nearest man's spine and fired.

As the bullet impacted the brave jerked and lay twitching against the cold earth, the blood flowing from him. The two nearby braves immediately made a dash for cover, but Ruff, anticipating that, managed to get lead into a second Kiowa. The heavy .44 bullet took him on the hip and shattered his leg. He folded up in midstride and went down on his face.

Suddenly it was still. The night which had seemed warm in the urgency of the moment now turned bitterly cold. Ruff stood pressed against the dark trunk of an oak, holding Sarah there too, not wanting to outline himself against the lighter background.

Kesselring's gun had fallen silent, probably because he had run out of targets but the man could be down, wounded or dead. Of George Birch there was not a sign, and thinking back Ruff couldn't recall seeing him at all during the attack or even hearing his gun. Possibly Birch had gone down before the first wave.

"Are they gone?" Sarah blurted out before Ruff could silence her. Didn't the woman realize how far sound carried out here?

If there were Kiowas still in the oak grove, they now knew exactly where Ruff and Sarah were. Move or stay? Ruff made his decision quickly.

With gestures he indicated to Sarah that they were going to try for the wagon. By circling through the scrub oak along the perimeter of the grove they could draw nearer, but still there would be a fifty-yard dash across open ground to be made.

It was that or stay in the woods, and now, Ruff felt sure, the Kiowas knew where to find them. He took a deep, slow breath and nodded to Sarah.

The brush scraped at their bare skin, but they moved quietly through the tangled shadows, staying in a crouch, eyes searching the darkness, hearts thudding in their chests. Ruff glanced back, saw the woman behind him, noticed with discomfort that her skin showed a gleaming white in the pale moonlight.

He stopped suddenly, so suddenly that Sarah bumped into him. There was something ahead in the brush. He knew it, although he hadn't heard anything or seen anything on a conscious level. It was a more primitive instinct alerting him—a wrong shadow, a scent, something he could not distinguish, but which had sent a chill crawling up his spine.

And then there was something to be seen. Birch, standing in the shadows, and before Ruff could react he fired the pistol he held in his hand point-blank.

Ruff felt the whoosh of a bullet past his ear, saw the puff of black-powder smoke, the flash illuminating Birch's long face. The roar of the gun rattled his eardrums, and then Sarah shrieked; the Kiowa who had been within feet of them was slumped to the earth, practically on her heels.

Birch was smiling thinly, knowing what Ruff had thought. Without speaking the man crouched and handed over a bundle of clothes to Justice, his own clothes and Sarah's.

Sarah managed to blush by moonlight as she held her dress and petticoats against her breasts, but Birch looked away, interested only in safety now.

The clearing was empty, moon-frosted. Birch looked at Ruff, and Ruff nodded. Bunching their muscles, they sprinted for the wagon, drawing a single shot from the trees near the river. But they made it, Sarah finishing in a slipping slide which landed her on her pale, bare rump.

Kesselring was there, and he looked up, shook his head in wonder, and peered toward the woods.

"They pulled off, I think, Ruff," he said.

"Looks like it."

"We kinda had them unintentionally in a crossfire. They must've thought we was pretty smart." Kesselring didn't smile, but there was dry humor in his eyes. "Birch went out looking for you. I couldn't stop him."

"Good thing you didn't," Ruff said. "And thanks, Birch. I apologize for thinking it was me you were shooting at."

"Not this time," Birch said, and he rose and strode away, holstering his pistol.

"You two got a problem?" Kesselring asked, watching Birch go.

"Of some kind. I don't know what started it." Ruff was pulling on his pants. Glancing to the side, Kesselring saw Sarah slipping into her petticoats.

"You can't figure it out, Ruff?" Kesselring asked.

"Maybe you're right," Justice agreed, looking at Sarah. But it seemed not to be Sarah at all which nettled Birch —or rather, not jealousy about her. Why Ruff thought that he couldn't explain; it was an instinct, like the recognition of danger in the woods. If it wasn't Sarah, then what? John Kent? A determination to make sure Justice didn't get to Colorado? He just didn't know.

"Let's get this wagon up on four wheels," Kesselring suggested. Walking to their horses, they mounted and returned, pulling it upright with ropes tied to the frame of the wagon. It came down with a clatter and shuddered to rest.

Sarah, now dressed, but still shaken, came to Ruff when he had stepped down again. She put her arms around his waist and buried her face against his chest, and he could feel her trembling.

"That was terrible, just terrible. Will it happen again?"

"It might," Ruff had to tell her. "Do you want to go back?"

"To what? I've sold our house. There's nothing in Virginia for me now. The answer, I suppose, is yes. I do want to go back, but I can't. I won't." She sniffed and tossed her head, dabbing at her nose with a tiny handkerchief. "I thought they didn't attack at night," she said, seeming to regain her composure.

"Did you? A lot of people have thought that—it's had fatal results at times. The Indians won't make a mounted charge at night; that's just plain foolish. It's too easy to break a horse's leg. But a little infiltration, count some quick coup, take a scalp, sure they'll do it. What time is better for that kind of work?"

"I won't sleep again the rest of the way," Sarah said. But she touched her hair, brushed off her dress, and said dismally, "What a mess I must look," and Ruff knew she would be all right now.

"You get up in that wagon," he told her, kissing the tip of her nose. "I'll stand watch. You get some sleep. It's a long road ahead of us; you'll fall asleep and bounce off the wagon seat if you don't get your rest."

"I'll try." She sighed. Then she stretched her arms out to him, intertwining her hands behind his neck, and kissed him goodnight.

Ruff helped her into the wagon, heard her small sigh of unhappiness as she surveyed the shambles of the interior, and, smiling, he turned away. Walking to the cold campfire, he touched the coffeepot, found it warm enough, and poured himself a cup.

Kesselring looked as if he was set to sit up all night. Propped against a log, rifle in his lap, he glanced at Ruff and sighed, shaking his head. Probably the Kiowas had had enough. Most likely it was a small band of young bucks out hunting who had decided it was time for a little war play. Probably they had decided it wasn't worth it. Probably—maybe.

Ruff walked back to the wagon, and there he sat, leaning up against the off wheel so that he could face away from Kesselring. Birch was nowhere in sight again.

He had followed them into the woods, had he? And for what purpose? Ruff wondered. He also wondered if just maybe Birch hadn't been laying for him, planning to kill him, when the sudden appearance of the Kiowa triggered an instinctive response. He wondered, but there was no way of knowing. All he did know was that he would keep Birch in front of him as much as possible from here on out.

Gold seeker, jealous lover, bodyguard—whichever he

was, Birch had shown himself to be dangerous. Pondering the man's identity, Ruff found himself wondering with sudden puzzlement if it was possible, barely possible, that George Birch was himself James Kent. That would explain a lot of things—how he happened to be on the boat with Sarah, why he was traveling with them, why he wanted Ruff Justice out of the way . . . but it just didn't fit tightly. Who then? Who? It plagued him, and he sat there the night through, turning it first one way and then the other, finally giving it up as false dawn grayed the eastern horizon and Kesselring stirred to life, making ready for another long day's travel.

By midmorning the skies to the north and west had begun to cloud up, and by noon great anvil-headed thunderclouds dominated the land. The wind was hard on their right shoulders, the grass trembling before it.

When the rain came it came with a crash of thunder and pitchforks of white lightning, and within minutes they were drenched to the bone, plodding onward blindly through the steel mesh of slanting rain.

The wind raked the plains and the rain streamed down. The world had gone dark and cold. It was impossible. Kesselring got near enough to Justice to shout above the howl of the wind, "We've got to put up somewhere."

"First spot you find!" Ruff agreed. He had to shout it twice before Kesselring heard him above the roar. Already, Ruff noticed, the ground was turning to red, oozing mud and the wagon was sliding through it, cutting foot-deep trenches as the oxen plodded forward.

Kesselring kept his eyes peeled, but there was little to choose from in the way of campsites. The water was beginning to run heavily in the washes, and there was no safe traveling for the time being, so he chose the highest ground he could find and left it at that.

The knoll was washed with rain, and the low clouds, heavy and dark, shut out the light of day as the thunder rumbled across the plains.

They staked out the horses and settled in to wait it out. Hunched together on the lee side of the wagon, the two plainsmen watched the lightning crackle across the black skies, watched the frothing silver-white water roar down the gullies which hours before had been bone-dry. The air was fresh with the rain, electric and sultry.

"If this keeps up long, we'll be stopped good and proper," Kesselring shouted to Ruff. The water ran off the guide's tattered hat. His beard hung in damp strands. "No gettin' across them gulches until they quit runnin'."

"As long as it doesn't turn to snow," Ruff answered, and Kesselring nodded grim agreement. These fall storms had a way of doing that, too. Raining to beat the band one minute, and the next, as the mass of Canadian air reached onto the plains, driving hailstorms or heavy snow. A good blizzard would freeze the wagon in its tracks, leaving them in a dangerous position indeed.

"Think I'd better check on Miss Kent," Ruff said, rising. The wind lifted his dark hair and his face was glossed with rain, but he never even smiled. Kesselring had to admire that.

"Might be a good idea," the big man said.

"Hello." Ruff peered under the tent flap and then crawled on in at Sarah's beckoning. The wind fluttered the canvas around them, pressing the fabric hard against the iron hoops. Sarah was dressed in a clean white blouse, unadorned gray skirt, and soft kid boots. She was trying to manage the small iron stove.

"The wind keeps forcing the soot back down the pipe," she said, pushing back a strand of dark hair with the back of her hand. "And the fire keeps going out."

"Those things aren't much use," Ruff said, shaking his head at the black stovepipe which passed through the canvas overhead through a specially designed collar. "Man that thought these up should have been shot. They've set a lot of wagons on fire, and that's about it."

"Mr. Birch thought we should have one," Sarah said

with disappointment as she prodded the fire again. "They're for weather like this, you know, when you can't cook outside."

Ruff only nodded, squatting on his heels, tipping his hat back. These patent stoves, too small to cook on and too heavy for overland travel, had made someone a fortune.

"Damn," she muttered as she burned her fingers. She sucked on her thumb, examined the burn, and then in disgust threw the poker down. "Well, it *seemed* like a good idea."

"If it lets up by morning we should make Kit Carson by tomorrow evening," Ruff said. Sarah watched him, waiting for him to go on.

"Kit Carson," he said, "that's the first town we'll hit in Colorado. The thing is, you haven't gotten around to telling us exactly where we are headed."

"Haven't I?" She laughed, moving closer to Ruff. She bent low and kissed his cheek lightly, her scent sweet, faint, enticing. "Well, it wasn't necessary," she said quickly. "My family will be meeting me at Kit Carson."

"You didn't say anything about that before, Sarah."

"No? I thought I told Mr. Kesselring that."

"You didn't."

"Well, now you know, so it doesn't matter," Sarah said, and she got to her knees, facing Ruff, her hands resting on his knees. She bowed her head and kissed his hand, her eyes sparkling, lusty. Those beautiful, deep-blue, lying eyes.

"Who exactly is there to meet you, Sarah?" Ruff asked, trying to keep his voice casual. It was difficult for more reasons than one. She had leaned far forward, and now her lips moved across his cheek and she nibbled at his ear, her breath steamy, gentle. Her hands kneaded his thighs.

"Who?" he repeated.

"Are you worried about me?" she asked with a toss of her head.

"Yes, I am."

"You don't have to be, Mr. Justice," she said, and she said it in a whisper, into his ear, as her hands ran up his thighs and to his crotch.

"I'd like to know, Sarah," Ruff said, gripping both of her wrists. She pulled away, startled.

"All right," she said slowly, her eyes filled with mingled indefinable emotions. Her breast heaved with the same emotions. "There's Uncle William and Aunt Clara," she said placidly. "They've been raising horses, I believe. Somewhere in the mountains behind Pueblo—you see, I don't actually know where it is, that's why I haven't told you.

"Aunt Clara and Uncle William."

"That's right, from Richmond. And my cousins Bobby and Ned are there, of course. And there's another cousin, Robert and his wife who run a stage depot near Pueblo—I think it's Pueblo." She laughed, not very effectively. "In fact, darn near the entire family has moved out here."

"And they're going to meet you in Kit Carson."

"Well, *someone* is, Ruff," she said, reverting to a Virginia drawl. "So don't you worry about me, darlin'. Let's just make the most of what's left of our journey, shall we?" Her lips met his, and it was difficult to say no, to disbelieve her tale, but he did.

"I promised Kesselring that I'd make a tour of the area, make sure there aren't any Kiowas around," he told her, inventing an excuse which would be effective with Sarah. She still shuddered every time someone said "Kiowa."

She drew away from him suddenly, all those mingled emotions drawing together to become a very real fear. "But they wouldn't be out there, would they? In this rain?"

"Best cover for sneaking around," Ruff told her, his eyes earnest.

"Well, I guess you have to."

"I do," he said. He rose and kissed her apologetically. Then he turned and slipped out into the rain, Sarah watching him from the upraised flap for a moment.

"I'm going out," he told Kesselring. The big man lifted his bushy eyebrows.

"Oh?"

Ruff had hefted his saddle and sodden blanket. Now he looked around. "Where's Birch?"

"Haven't seen him for an hour or so. Maybe he favors riding out in the rain, too," Kesselring said with a bare smile.

"Could be. Try not to get washed away, Wade. I'll be back in an hour or so."

"Suit yourself," Kesselring said. He was fishing in his pocket for chewing tobacco—the pipe was hopeless in the downpour. The old scout asked no more questions, figuring that Ruff's business was his own. He was a good man, was Wade Kesselring, a fighting man, a man with warm good humor, dry wit, and a sense of his own place in the world. He had been up the river and over the mountains. He had seen the elephant and laughed at it. He was a comfort to have around.

Ruff saddled his chestnut horse. The animal rolled morose eyes at him as he swept the water from its back, threw on the water-heavy saddle blanket, and smoothed it.

"I don't feel like it any more than you do," Ruff said to the horse. But he had told Sarah he was going out—he had to do it. Any Kiowa with half a brain was holed up in some warm spot with a woman, but Ruff wanted the time to think.

None of it fit, not correctly. Birch was a liar; Sarah Kent told only half the truth. Tomorrow, or the next day at the latest, they would reach Kit Carson. And then what? There was no inconspicuous way for Ruff to hang around the town waiting to see who did come to pick her up, no way to follow her to her destination.

The rain poured down, stinging Ruff's back through his buckskins. The horse moved forward miserably, its head lowered. The rivers ran past, raging and frothing, and thunder rattled across the plains.

He had told Wade Kesselring he'd be gone awhile, but he had had plenty of this weather already, and the thoughts were still jumbled, unclear in his mind. He couldn't shake loose the answers he needed to have.

"Come on, old boy," he told the chestnut, stroking its wet, cold neck. "Let's head on back."

The wind was at his back now. Lightning briefly, starkly illuminated the plains, and in the flash of light he could see the small, dark form of the wagon. Then the lightning flickered out and the world went dark as sin again. The horse misstepped, in a prairie dog hole, Ruff thought, regained its stride, and plodded on. The wind worked in its mane and lifted its tail.

Cold it was, growing colder, and Ruff began to wonder if it wasn't going to snow before darkness fell. He found the wagon, walked his horse around it, and stopped cold.

It was Kesselring, and he wasn't moving. Splayed out against the cold, damp earth he lay there, the rain in his face, his mouth trickling blood, an arrow projecting from his throat.

Ruff moved to him, Colt in his hands, eyes peering through the rain which washed down, brushing his hair across his face. Dead. Kesselring was dead, the arrow buried deep in his throat, the rain washing away the blood which flowed away from the wound.

Ruff stepped to the tailgate of the wagon and peered in. Nothing. Sarah was gone. All the horses were gone. There was no sign of George Birch.

And no sign of a battle, despite the arrow in Kesselring. Ruff moved back to the body, wiping the rain from his face. He crouched down. Kesselring's rifle was across his lap, unfired. Ruff opened the big man's shirt, finding a second wound, and he nodded with grim understanding.

That arrow hadn't been shot into Kesselring, but driven in by hand. They had tried the chest first, but it had glanced off a rib. The second choice, the throat, had worked all too well.

Ruff grabbed the loose reins to the chestnut, and with his Colt still in his hand he circled the camp, trying to read some sense into the rain-blurred confusion of tracks. It was impossible to tell much. Three horses—or four—heading west, one deep indentation of a boot heel which might or might not have been George Birch's. Lightning flickered across the dark skies as Ruff swung into leather, his eyes as hot as the white bolt of lightning, his face as sullen as the low, black clouds.

He startled the chestnut by heeling it into a run, aiming it toward the wash ahead, which ran water from bank to bank now. A mad, foaming stream running with the force of locomotives, but they had gotten across it somehow.

Ruff turned his horse northward, lost the sign and picked it up again, finding where they had crossed. The wash narrowed considerably as it forced its way between two massive, water-cut boulders which formed a stony chute. Foam washed over the flattened tops of the boulders, but it was possible to leap a good horse over the gap.

That was just what Ruff meant to do. Backing the chestnut, he tightened the grip his knees had on the horse's ribs, heeled it into motion, and hoped the horse was a jumper.

The chestnut showed no hesitation. He took off in a smooth, powerful jump as the water raged on. It was a jump which was never completed.

The rifle roared out of the storm-dark day, as loud as thunder, and Ruff felt the impact as the bullet thudded into the horse's shoulder, narrowly missing his knee.

The horse folded up, slammed roughly, clumsily, into the far bank, and flopped onto its side as the rifle roared again. Or was it thunder this time? Ruff couldn't even be sure.

The horse writhed beneath him, made a feeble attempt to claw at the bank, which was rain-slick stone, failed, and fell, rolling Ruff off its back.

Justice leaped free, not wanting the chestnut to fall on him. He grabbed for his Henry rifle, missed, and dove away, instantly hitting the icy thrust of the roaring river. He was sucked down, tossed around, and dashed against a hidden rock.

He managed to claw his way to the surface and take a deep saving breath before he was rolled over again, the wild river tossing him about like a twig as the day darkened still more, becoming a tossing, frothing blackness as if the sky reflected the turgid flood of the river.

It was cold, desperately cold. Ruff fought to stay on the surface. The rain had begun to fall in hard sheets, beating with a rage against the river. The banks slid past, mocking Ruff's attempt to reach them, and he thought briefly of the Missouri. He hadn't drowned then. He had saved himself—only to cross five hundred miles of dry land to drown in some storm-washed gully.

His buckskins were saturated; it was like wearing a suit of lead. But there was no thought of taking them off, no time for that, little time for thought.

The river tumbled him again. His head narrowly missed a bobbing uprooted cottonwood tree. He tried to cling to it, found it as easy as grabbing hold of a bull's horns, and gave up.

The river was narrowing again, and by the time he had seen possible salvation he was already to it. He was driven into the narrow outcropping which projected from the sandy bluff above. Slammed into it so hard that he felt a rib crack, felt the breath driven from his tortured chest. But he managed to hang on, to cling to the rock, to crawl up onto it as the river, loud in his ears, rolled on, as thunder boomed across the plains.

He crawled up onto it and found he had the strength to do no more. He sat there, head hanging heavily, hair across his face, sitting in the freezing darkness, listening to the roar of the river, the crackling of the storm, as night fell and the world became a black, booming, watery hell where nothing moved but the awesome tangled forces of nature. He drew up his knees and rested his head on them, shivering miserably as the black night thundered on, as his enemies made their escape and Wade Kesselring lay, eyes open to the cold night and the rain. He sat there unmoving, but he found he was no longer cold. There was a hot rage building in him, a flaring, violent rage which swept aside all of the darkness, the cold, leaving Ruff with only a single, demanding emotion. He would find the man who did this. Find him and kill him where he stood.

# 5.

Dawn was a fan of beaten gold through the fractured gray clouds which roofed over the earth. The wind was steady, the river rushed on. Justice stretched stiffly. He was chilled to the bone, bruised and weary. He sat for a long hour looking at the river, which was slate gray now, filmed with the white froth of motion. The skies paled. The high clouds took on a brief, deep violet tone and the long grass plains flushed pink.

Ruff rose finally, his knee buckling under him at his first attempt. He looked up and saw the steep, sandy bank which rose from the nearly flat, rocky outcropping where he now rested. Not much of a climb at all—for a man who was fresh and able. To Ruff just then it looked like a mountain.

He began to climb. The bluffs were loose sand, given to sagging and caving in with each movement Ruff made. Handholds were difficult to rely on, but fifteen minutes' work brought him up and over the bluff. He lay against the grassy, muddy earth for a minute, gasping for breath, and then he stood, striding northward, a tall, lean, dark-haired man in wet buckskins.

He had been carried even farther south than he suspected. It was two hours before he found the camp. Wade Kesselring still sat there, watching Ruff's approach with open eyes. The mule, ground-tethered not far from the wagon, brayed at him. It had cropped all the grass within the radius of its tether.

Ruff pulled up the peg and led the mule aside, tethering it again. Then he returned to Kesselring.

There was no shovel in the wagon, no useful tool of any sort, and so he kicked and pried a plank from the tailgate, and with that poor implement he scraped a shallow, muddy grave for one of the rightest men who ever rode the long plains.

Then Ruff cut the oxen free. They would fare well enough. They were too big for the wolves to bother, and the grass was high.

That done, Ruff walked back to the mule. "You ever been ridden, old-timer?" Ruff asked, walking slowly around the wary animal. The mule flattened its ears and sidestepped.

"Take it easy," he said, stroking the white muzzle.

Fashioning a hackamore from a length of hemp, he slipped it over the mule's head, the animal protesting only a little. It kicked out once, but that seemed to be out of surprise and not anger.

Settling the big Missouri mule, Justice swung aboard, and surprisingly the mule had no real objections. It minded the reins with only a little obstinacy, and Justice turned it westward, Wade Kesselring's big Sharps .50 in his hand, his face set grimly.

There was no jumping the gully on the mule, but a few hours north Justice found a ford of sorts. The water went to the mule's belly, but it seemed not to mind. It plodded steadily onward, toward Kit Carson and the Rocky Mountains beyond, which had their heads buried in the dissipating clouds, a bulwark against encroachment, a stunning reminder of man's smallness.

Ruff rode toward the south and west, hoping to cut some kind of sign, but the rain had swept away any such chance. It was possible that Birch and Sarah hadn't headed for Kit Carson at all, but there was nowhere else.

They were traveling with few supplies now, and they would have to stop somewhere. Kit Carson it was—the town, a collection of slovenly shacks, patched tents, a few frame buildings, unpainted and weather-grayed, one yellow brick structure and a white, steepled church set in the center of town, rose up from the sodden surrounding plains and took on form, color, reality.

They would be there, had to be, and they would be waiting.

The streets of Kit Carson were muddy, the air cool when Ruff Justice rode into the unvarnished frontier town. Heads turned to study him as he rode up the main street, hatless, astride a lanky, long-eared mule; his hair hung wildly across face and shoulders, his buckskins were steaming as the sun dried them on his back. A man in a town suit turned his wife away from this apparition.

Ruff's eyes searched the town. Two new wagons were being loaded in front of the emporium, and a checker game was in progress on the veranda of the white, weathered hotel at the corner. A Mexican dozed in front of the saloon, where a voice was raised in laughter. But there was no sign of George Birch, his horse, or Sarah Kent.

He rode directly to the only stable in town and stepped stiffly from the mule. The sleepy-eyed hostler looked at him from under bushy white eyebrows, then rose from his three-legged stool, stretching expansively.

"Help you?"

"I want to put the mule up and buy a horse from you, if you've got anything suitable."

"I've got what you see," the hostler answered, waving an arm. "Have a look around."

Ruff did so, and then casually asked his question. "I wonder if you've seen my partner. He rode in earlier." Justice described the man and the horse. The hostler shook his head.

"There's been no strangers in town today, nor yesterday for that matter. Nor the day before that I can recollect," he answered, removing his battered hat to scratch his head.

"Is there another stable in town?"

"Can't find a horse you like? Did you see the palomino?" The hostler started walking back toward the leggy gelding.

"It's not that. I just wondered if maybe my partner had stopped somewhere else."

"There's no other stable, mister."

"Is there a ranch nearby?"

The hostler's eyes narrowed. He wagged his head again. "Not for twenty miles, and that's Clara Tuck way up on Widow Creek." He added, "And I don't think your partner would head up that way."

"Why not?" Ruff asked. The stableman ignored his question.

"How about that blue roan? He's nine years old, but steady, with a lot of chest on him. Good mountain horse."

"Why wouldn't he head up to Widow Creek?" Ruff persisted.

"Why would he? Just Mrs. Tuck up there. She's got no horses. She ain't got much, as far as that goes. No reason anybody would go up there."

"Is there anyplace else?"

"Mister," the hostler said in some exasperation, "there's whatever you want. A few gold claims, a timber company, a stage stop, a man running sheep . . . but goddam, if you don't know where your partner's heading, I can't very well help you by mappin' out the whole territory. You need a horse or not?"

"I need a horse," Ruff said with a faint smile. "How much for the blue roan?"

It took fifteen minutes of dickering. The hostler agreed to throw in a new set of shoes, and Ruff paid him fifty dollars for the solid-looking blue roan.

Another fifty dollars of army money. The expenditures

were going to take a lot of justifying to General Hightower, but that didn't bother Ruff. What did bother him was the idea that he might have to report that he had lost Sarah Kent again. With no leads it looked bleak. Kent, apparently with Birch's help, had swooped down and taken his sister away. Justice had lost the trail, and there was little hope of finding it again. The man had all of Colorado to hide in.

Kit Carson had one hotel, the Grand, and two boardinghouses. Ruff checked through them, asking after Sarah Kent. No one had seen her, or if anyone had he wouldn't admit it.

At the Grand, Justice had noticed the clerk nod, and glancing over his shoulder he saw a big man with a huge black beard watching silently from a corner chair. What, if anything, it had to do with him, Ruff couldn't be sure.

By noon he had turned the town inside out, asking at the general stores, the boardinghouses, the stables. Nothing. If Sarah Kent had come into this town, she had done it in utter secrecy. Justice was beginning to doubt that she had come here at all.

If the man who had met them had been carrying supplies, there had been no need to come into Kit Carson. They could have veered south toward Pueblo, north toward Denver, any of a hundred places. Ruff walked along the ribbon of shade offered by the awning above the plank walk, and his eyes lifted to the far, towering mountains.

The great jumbled mass of the deep-blue Rocky Mountains, snowcapped, ominous. He wondered how in the hell you ever got a man back out of a fortress like that.

His stomach was complaining loudly, and Ruff crossed the street, letting a freight wagon pass, spuming up yellow dust. The restaurant he entered was half of a building which also contained a long bar and a few card tables. The rooms, undivided except for a low iron railing, presented a strong contrast.

The restaurant section had small square tables with checkered tablecloths, a waxed hardwood floor, and frilly curtains at the windows. The saloon had sawdust sprinkled on a rough plank floor, the windows painted over in blue and yellow, and a squalid atmosphere.

The eating seemed to be over for the day, the drinking just beginning. The restaurant had only a single customer, an older, whiskered man who was wiping his bread through egg yolk. The bar of the saloon was lined with rough, dirty men. Miners, cowboys, drifters soaking up cheap whiskey and green beer as fast as it could be poured.

Ruff took a table and waited for the slow-moving blond waitress to appear from the kitchen. Almost with exasperation she found a crudely printed menu and walked to Ruff's table.

"Still breakfast time?" he asked with a smile.

"Whatever you want," she said wearily.

She stood on one foot, hip cocked, bagged eyes watching Justice, who finally said, "Eggs, ham, potatoes, coffee."

Without writing it down she took the cardboard menu and stumped back toward the kitchen. Ruff smiled to himself, ran fingers through his tangled dark hair, and glanced idly at the saloon.

The men were most serious about their drinking. No one looked at him or even spoke much. Drinking, it seemed, was a solemn affair in Kit Carson, Colorado. Ruff had started to look away when the man in the shadows caught his eye. This one was looking at Ruff, although his eyes shifted away as Justice glanced at him. It was the big man with the black beard, the man from the hotel.

Ruff frowned, looked up and nodded his thanks as the waitress slapped down a steaming platter and a quart pot of coffee, and began to eat.

Now Black Beard was talking to two other men. One

young, blond, greasy. The other dark, Mexican probably, with a pocked face. Their faces were insolent, challenging. Ruff ignored them and got down to eating.

Now and then he looked up. The men hadn't shifted an inch. The Mexican, boot heel hooked over the bar rail, elbows on the counter, his face half hidden by a bushy mustache. The blond kid, his mouth open partway, revealing crooked, yellow teeth, and Black Beard, immense through the chest, but giving the impression of slackness. A strong man going rapidly to flab.

Ruff pushed away his platter, poured a third cup of black coffee, and leaned back in his chair, sighing.

He knew what was coming; he could smell it. But why?

The three men stood at the end of the bar priming themselves with liquor. It was a game they had to play, a dangerous game. A remark, a comment taken as an insult, a hard, challenging glare. They wanted a fight, and they would have it.

It was the sort of thing Justice usually avoided at all costs. Ordinarily it was decent men who played these barroom games. Men who were honest, hard-working, friendly until liquor brought their deep frustrations to the surface. It seemed a shame to kill a man in those circumstances.

But these three—Ruff doubted that it was a game with them. It appeared to be a job, pure and simple. Take the man down; and they would try it.

He stood, dropped two silver dollars on the table, and strode toward the door, knowing he would never make it that far. And he didn't; they instantly angled toward him, and Ruff's lip twitched. He glanced at them, trying to gauge them. Could they be talked out of it, bluffed away, ignored? He didn't think so. No, this was a business deal. The big Sharps rifle was cool, comforting in his hand. He only hoped he didn't have to use it. A Sharps .50 could blow a hole the size of a man's head through a buffalo.

What it would do to a man in close quarters was not pleasant to ponder.

"Hey, squaw man!" Black Beard called, his voice a jeer. Ruff stopped, shaking his head. They would have their fight no matter the consequences. He turned slowly to face the damned fools.

"Did you want something?" he asked mildly.

"Did you want something?" the yellow-haired kid said mockingly. "We want your ass, mister."

"Oh? Things that lonely in this town?" Ruff asked with hardly a smile. The kid twitched and started forward. Black Beard's hand fell on his shoulder.

"No need to insult folks," Black Beard said, moving his bulk nearer to Ruff, cutting him off from the door. The Mexican hadn't spoken. He lounged against the wall beside the door, thumbs hooked into his gunbelt.

"No need to keep this up," Ruff replied. Black Beard started to reply, then shut up. There was some warning in those blue eyes of Ruff Justice, some warning sign as clear as the menace in a rattler's twitching tail. The blond kid didn't see it—maybe he had never heard a rattler or looked into a panther's eyes.

"Ain't you the son of a bitch that come into town ridin' a jackass?" he asked, his gaping mouth slackening still more, his stale scent in Ruff's nostrils.

"That animal was no jack," Ruff told him. "He's been cut. How about you, boy?"

The kid's expression didn't change for a minute. Then he stiffened as if he'd been slapped. "What're you callin' me?" he demanded.

"Did I offend you, sonny?" Ruff asked mildly. "I'm sorry. I just wondered if a man who needs to gang up three against one like this *is* a man. Seemed like you might be missing some necessary equipment. Matter of fact," he said, glancing at the Mexican, "I wouldn't bet there's a pair of balls between the three of you."

Ruff was pushing it and pushing it hard, but he didn't

care just then. These men had come to push him into a fight, to maim and batter him no matter what he said or did; he might as well get a few jibes in. For whatever reason, the barb had set deep in the blond kid. He was pale, trembling. And he flagged it as he went for his gun.

Justice had the Sharps by its barrel, and as the kid made his move he simply swung it up and out. Up and out and down with all of his strength behind it. The stock of the Sharps rifle smashed into the kid's jaw, and he went down, his pistol clattering free, his face awash with blood.

Black Beard had gone for his weapon as well, but a second too late. Ruff had his own Colt in his hand, and Black Beard froze. The Mexican, leaning against the wall beside the door, was slow to react. He pawed at his pistol, worn for a cross draw, and it was just too slow.

Ruff reached for the open door and swung it viciously. The Mexican, his gun coming free of leather, was caught by the solid edge of the oak door. It slammed into the center of his dark face, and his knees buckled. He staggered forward one step before sagging against the wall, his nose broken, his pistol lying on the floor beside his limp hand.

Black Beard, trembling with rage or fear or both, faced Justice, his hand on his gun, Ruff's pistol covering him. "Go ahead," Ruff taunted him. These men had his blood up. It was no laughing matter when folks tried to kill you. It stirred Ruff to red-eyed anger. He wasn't ready to die yet, and that's what these men had wanted. Angrily he stuffed his pistol back into his holster and stepped forward, face to face with the bearded man.

"Draw that weapon, mister," Ruff challenged. The big man backed away; he was still reading those cold blue eyes right.

"No. It's over, let it be." He took his Colt out gingerly and threw it across the room. The waitress and a Chinese cook stood gawking at the scene.

Justice stepped nearer, following the big man as he backed away, his dark, watery eyes shifting from side to side as if searching for a path of escape. Black Beard's back came up against the wall and Ruff stepped in closer, drawing his Bowie from the sheath at the back of his belt.

"Now look here . . . what are you going to do?" Black Beard asked, his voice a thin whine. The Mexican, holding his head and sitting up, was moaning.

"I want to know who sent you," Ruff said.

"No one—we were just having some fun."

"Who?" Ruff had his knife beneath Black Beard's chin now.

"Nobody!" he squawked, and Ruff knew in that minute that the man wasn't going to talk. He was more afraid of whoever had sent him than of anything Ruff might threaten to do.

"Stay away from me," Ruff said softly. "Just stay away." As he spoke he took Black Beard's whiskers in his left hand and sawed through them with his Bowie. He stepped back holding a handful of beard. "You hear me? Next time it won't be something that'll grow back."

"I hear you," Black Beard said. He was no longer whining. A small crowd from the saloon had gathered, and Ruff heard a chuckle behind his back. The big man stood there with his whiskers chopped off in a ragged line, and his eyes had gone cold. They smoldered as they studied Ruff, and Justice knew this man would not forget him. He had injured his pride.

Well, good, he thought. The man asked for it, and he's come out damned lucky. He looked at the chin whiskers in his hand and muttered, "I must be going soft." Then, sheathing his knife, he dropped the handful of greasy beard, snatched up the Sharps, and shouldered past the big man. For good luck he snapped the door open again and heard the Mexican sigh as it slammed into his face once more.

The street was hot, dusty, nearly empty. The town

looked neglected, as if it was dying and didn't know it. Justice hadn't liked this town from first glance; now he wanted to be away from it as soon as possible.

He bought a new hat, a dark-gray, wide-brimmed felt, at the emporium, returned to pick up the newly shod blue roan and his pack mule, and rode westward out of Kit Carson before an hour had passed.

He rode slowly over the green hills, taking in the flourish of color the wildflowers spattered against the grass, the winking quicksilver of a narrow rill catching the sunlight, the pleasant, melodic sound of a meadowlark singing.

It was damned fine country, a damned fine day, but Justice couldn't enjoy it for long. He stepped down close up against a stand of blue spruce at the edge of a broad meadow and let the animals drink.

"What now, Ruffin T.?" he asked himself. He stood, hands on hips, watching the meadow, the deep forests, the brown patch which was Kit Carson seen through the broken ranks of trees below him.

What now indeed. He was in Colorado, and so supposedly was the killer, James Kent. End of what he knew.

Ruff filled his canteens, sagged into the shade of the pine trees, and sat for a time, smelling the sweet grass, the faintly spiced air. He tried to sort out what he knew.

Kent wasn't in Kit Carson, but there were two very good reasons for thinking he, or at least Sarah, had been there. First of all, it was the only town for miles, and probably they would have needed supplies. Maybe not, but there was a good chance.

The second reason was more solid. Three men set up to beat Ruff Justice. Why? A barroom game. Maybe, but these three had gone out of their way to start trouble, and Black Beard had spotted him earlier in the hotel. No, that was no coincidence.

The inescapable conclusion was that Kent had been through Kit Carson. Not only that, he was known there.

How else could he have found three men like those to hire?

"Where's that leave me?" Ruff looked at the blue roan, which was studying him curiously, and then he suddenly broke out laughing. It left him absolutely nowhere. "You should've been a Pinkerton detective, son," he told himself, still laughing.

But thinking it over again, he decided that Kent was probably a local. Why not circle the area and talk to folks, see what came up? He decided to try it, and if he dead-ended, learning nothing in a week or so, he would just have to swallow his pride, pack it in, and wire Hightower that he had failed.

He would hate to have to send that wire. Ruff recalled the anger in the general's words, the righteous lust for revenge. It would gall Hightower the rest of his life if Kent got away after murdering Hightower's men. The gold was hardly mentioned, and Justice knew the general didn't give a damn about it. That was a matter of accounting. The blood that had flowed—that was a matter of honor, an entirely different matter. A good commander expected a lot from his men, but by God he was with them when there was trouble. Hightower felt he had let those men down. They were more than numbers to him; they were faces and they were his responsibility. A man like Hightower didn't take his responsibility lightly.

Nor did a man like Ruffin T. Justice.

He rode higher into the mountains, through incredibly beautiful deep valleys studded with cedar and spruce. The sun glinted behind the spires of the mountain peaks, outlining their shattered ridges with pure gold briefly before early dusk settled into the valleys.

He found a larger creek where the quick-running water made bright appealing sounds as it rushed over the streambed rocks.

Ruff splashed across the creek in the dusky light and climbed the far bank, which was rife with wild fern and dogwood. Beyond the screen of brush he found a wagon trail. It was obviously seldom used; weeds grew up around old, deep ruts.

Turning westward, toward the shadowed mountains, he began looking for a spot to camp. Night was coming in rapidly, and he was new to this country. Below him the creek plunged downslope through deep brush. The first star was winking on above the mountains, shining through a frail, faintly purple pennant of clouds.

Ruff crested the saddleback and sat overlooking a deeper, wider valley, deep in shadow. Smoke rose in a thin, wind-tortured spiral from the stone chimney of a cabin a quarter of a mile below.

He hesitated and then rode that way. The cabin was dark despite the signs of habitation. The pole corrals held a single horse, although they had been designed for many more animals. The grass was long in the meadow.

Someone had planted an elm not far from the stone-walled well beyond the stables, but the tree had long ago died. The house, the ranch, was a curious mixture of vitality and decay, as if it had been a living, blossoming thing strangled in its vigor.

Ruff rode slowly across the long valley toward the squat, sod-roofed house. He carried the Sharps across the withers of the roan, ready to be used if necessary, but there seemed little likelihood of that. The house was silent, the valley deep and peaceful at this hour. Ruff found a road which led to the front door of the house, passing through a stand of very old pines, and he swung the roan that way.

The mule balked, and he gave a tug on the tow line, wondering what perversity in man's nature had caused him to ever try domesticating this recalcitrant creature.

He tilted his head up, saw the blanket of blue-white stars, saw the tips of the dark pines swaying in the gentle wind . . . and then he felt the white-hot impact of a bullet, the searing pain, and moments later he heard the roar of a rifle, but by then he was falling, falling helplessly to the hard, cold earth beneath him.

The roan danced away in panic, the pack mule brayed and leaped into the air, and Ruff Justice lay against the earth, blood leaking from his chest, his thoughts scattered and broken, the rifle lying just out of reach, just beyond his fingers, which clawed shallow furrows in the earth as he reached for the Sharps, never quite grasping it.

The trees swam in dizzy, clouded circles overhead. His eyes were unfocused, his heart racing. Something hot and vital was flowing across his chest. Blinking away the pain and confusion, Ruff peered up and saw the black silhouette blotting out the diamond stars. A rifle muzzle was jabbed into his face, and a boot prodded him.

Then there was no more for a time. Ruff Justice lay on his back, blood leaking out of him, and he could not even see the face of his attacker; he did not even know who had killed him, and that angered him. But the anger was lost as the pit beneath him opened wide and he tumbled away down the long, long flight of velvet stairs into unconsciousness.

# 6.

THE SUNLIGHT STREAMING through the faded blue curtains struck his eyes like hot irons. Ruff had to turn his head away, and that small motion brought a protest of angry pain from his chest, and it all returned to him.

He had been shot. By whom, and why? Cautiously he lifted an eyelid, trying to place himself, to learn where he was, what had caused this.

He squinted toward the small window, watching the flat rays of sunlight, the suspended motes of dust dancing in the faint, vector-straight current of the sunbeam. There was nothing else on that wall, no clue as to where he was except the wall itself. Of unplaned planks, never painted, the wood was a deep grayish brown, backed with tarpaper. The ceiling, he saw by rolling his eyes, was even rougher, and he could see sod above the slats.

The wall before him encased a narrow, poorly made door. To his left a shabby bureau had been shoved up against the wall. A chipped washbasin and matching porcelain pitcher sat there.

And he was . . . Ruff Justice, wild-country scout, plainsman, somewhat notorious gunfighter, poet, adventurer, soldier, and dilettante, lying on a heavy bed on a mattress of straw ticking, his chest pinched with throbbing pain, his ankles and wrists tied to the bedposts. A prisoner.

Ruff twisted his head, fighting down the nausea produced by the accompanying pain. His wrist was wrapped with linen and then tied with heavy hemp. The rope was looped around the bedpost, tied competently and tightly.

A prisoner. Whose? He grimaced, shifted slightly, and stared at the door, and then he hollered. The expansion of his chest, the sudden exhalation, triggered violent pain. He laid his head back, amazed that the effort had caused his forehead to break out in beads of perspiration.

No one came. He watched the door expectantly, listened for the sound of footfalls, but no one came. He shouted again, with the same result. The house beyond the door remained silent. The sun beamed through the curtains. His chest rose and fell with his effortful breathing.

He blinked the perspiration from his eyes and tried to sort things out, but they wouldn't sort. He had been shot and was now a prisoner. But it couldn't have been Kent or George Birch who had shot him. It couldn't have been Black Beard and his cronies. None of them would have taken the time and trouble to bind up his wound, to place him on a bed in this tiny room.

They would have stood over him and shot him full of holes, left him for the coyotes and the buzzards.

Then who? He could summon no answer. He wanted to yell again, to scream out until someone came, no matter who, but it was too painful to yell, and so he lay there, his eyes alive, flickering, studying the ropes that bound him, the tiny sun-bright window.

He could move his left arm without the blinding pain flooding his brain, he had discovered, and he moved it now, tugging at the rope which held that arm, testing it gently at first, then more violently, twisting his wrist, straining against the knots which held him. He only managed to draw the knots tighter.

Panting, he lay back, watching the shadows slowly shift across the rough floor. He lay there until the last orange glint of light was washed away from the window and he was immersed in shadow, in silent pain.

An hour later he heard the horse drum up to the house, heard a door open and slam, and then, when the darkness was all but complete, the door to his room opened and he lifted his head, expecting . . . anything but the small blond woman who stood there in outsized man's clothing, holding a businesslike Winchester in her hands.

"Made it through the day, did you?" she muttered. "Well, I figured you would. Any man who survived at all."

"What happened to me?"

"Happened? I shot you!" she snapped, apparently proud of the fact.

The lanternlight from the outer room silhouetted her and cast an aura around her golden, frizzy hair. She wasn't young anymore, thirty perhaps, but she was trim, handsome in a stiff, unbending way.

"Why . . . ?" he started to ask, but she turned away, leaning the Winchester up against the wall.

"I'll spoon you up somethin' to eat if you think you can hold it down. If you don't, say so now. I don't want to clean it up."

"I think I can handle it," Ruff said. She didn't answer him. He could see into the lighted room beyond, see a rickety puncheon table, an old musket hanging on the wall above a stone fireplace, a slicker hung on a nail near the door. Of the woman he could see nothing.

But she made her presence known. In the unseen kitchen she banged away, slamming down pots, breathing dry muttered comments.

It was an hour before she reappeared, wearing a tattered apron over her twill pants and cotton shirt. Her expression hadn't softened a bit.

"I'll have to spoon it to you."

"You could untie me," he suggested.

"I could cut my own throat," she replied.

"What's the matter with you?" Ruff asked, growing angry.

"You! Got to nurse and feed you. My thanks for being too softhearted to finish you off."

"But why, lady . . . ?"

"You going to eat or not? I got things to do!"

Their eyes locked, and Ruff found no hint of softness in her gray, gold-flecked eyes. He sighed, feeling too weak to argue.

She sat down, her hip next to his waist, and began spooning the salty beef stew into his mouth. It was too hot, but she gave him no time to protest. One spoonful followed the other, and it was swallow or choke.

She stopped abruptly when the bowl was only half empty. "I reckon that's enough," she said, rising. Ruff, forgetting his hand was tied, started to grab her wrist. She noticed the gesture, half smiled, and stood looking down at him.

"I want to know what this is all about," Ruff said.

"I reckon you know," she replied shortly. Then, spinning, she walked out the door, slammed it behind her, and left him in deep, uncomfortable darkness.

The weakness caused by the wound in his chest made it possible for him to sleep. He awoke only once, sometime after midnight, and listening he thought he could make out the sound of voices in low conversation. But there was a rising wind, the first spattering sounds of rain, and he could not be sure. It might have been only the old house grumbling and creaking in protest.

She tramped in at dawn, a cup of coffee in her hands.

"You need attention?" she asked briskly.

"What do you mean?"

"You know what I mean—I don't want to have to clean up that bed."

"I'm all right."

"Good. Drink this coffee and I'll see to your wound. Maybe we're both lucky and you've got the gangrene."

"You're a pleasant wake-me-up," Ruff growled.

"I beat the devil, mister," she said. Testing the coffee with her finger, she decided it was too hot. "I'll look at that gunshot wound first."

Roughly then she unwound the bandaging. The bullet, Ruff could see now, had taken him at an extreme angle. She had damned near missed him. The slug had cut a deep, angry furrow across his chest muscle. She had stitched it up with heavy cotton thread—blue thread.

"It don't look bad," she said. "Can't hurt much."

"That's a matter of opinion."

She fingered the ugly purple-and-yellow bruising around the wound, saw Ruff wince, and belatedly asked, "Does that hurt?"

"It does hurt, lady, yes."

"Well, you'll make it. Live long enough to hang, probably." She stood, wiping her hands on her apron. "You run with the wrong crowd, mister."

"Justice."

"What?"

"My name is Justice, Ruffin T."

"That so. I'll see they get it right on your tombstone."

She lifted his head and poured some of the tepid coffee through his lips. He gagged on it. It was black as sin and tasted like lye. "I never was much of a hand at coffee. Old Lyle, he used to tell me . . ." Her voice faded away. Whatever it was old Lyle used to say, Ruff never discovered.

"Lady," he said as she was beginning to leave, "I want you to listen to me for one minute. I don't run with a gang of any kind. My name is Justice, Ruffin T. I'm working for the army—"

"Don't hand me that!"

"You can check it out. Wire General Hightower at Fort Towson down in the Indian Nation."

"We got no telegraph. I got no money."

"I have money!" Ruff told her in frustration. "Send a man to the nearest army post, use their wire."

"What kinda army business?" she asked suspiciously.

"Nothing to do with you or your problems," he answered. He thought he could see a chink in her defenses, and he pressed it. "You can do this for me. You've got the wrong man somehow, believe me."

"Mister, I could almost believe you . . . but I been lied to by too many men." With that she went out, closing the door behind her, and Ruff let his head sag slowly back onto the pillow.

He heard the woman stamp across the floor, saw her shoulder into a rain slicker and go out. The rain settled in and drummed on the roof as the sky beyond the window went dark. A small leak in the roof allowed an intermittent drop of water to fall to the floor at the foot of Ruff's bed.

He watched it as if hypnotized for half an hour. Then, anger building in him, he tried to tear his left hand free again. Failing that, he tried his feet. It was utter failure, and frustration took hold.

This damned silly woman had him prisoner. Wherever Sarah Kent had gone, she was a good deal farther down the trail now than she had been two days ago. If there had ever been any hope of finding her trail, the rain had just about eliminated that possibility.

He tried to sleep, and managed it for a while. When he awoke it was nearly nightfall again. The opening door had nudged him awake, and now, peering into the lanternlight, he could see that she had returned.

"Dinner," she said. Something about her had changed. She seemed softer, quieter. Ruff watched her as she approached the bed, sat on it, and looked directly into his eyes. "I . . . I'm afraid I've made a terrible mistake, Mr. Justice."

"You sent the wire?" No. She couldn't have gotten an answer so soon.

"No." She wagged her head. "But I thought about it. I rode into Kit Carson and talked to a man named Colly Higgins—you know him."

"No."

"He's a big man, a rough man with a black beard."

"Then I do know him, if that's Colly Higgins. Does he trim that beard a little oddly?"

She smiled faintly. "That's the man. He asked if I had seen you. 'A lanky, long-haired bastard carrying an old Sharps,' I believe he said."

"Flattering." ·

"Yes." The rain pattered down. Silver rivulets trickled across the frosted windowpane. "So then I knew, of course. Colly Higgins is one of Donovan's men, everyone knows that."

"Donovan?"

"He's the man . . . never mind. It doesn't matter now, does it? But when I found out that you and Colly Higgins had had a run-in, well, I knew you weren't what , . . I thought you were."

"One of Donovan's men."

"Yes." Defensively she asked, "Well, who else would ride up here on Widow Creek?"

"Then you're Clara Tuck."

She looked at him with puzzlement. "How did you know that?"

"The man at the stables told me that no one came up here, that a woman named Clara Tuck had a rather poor place up on Widow Creek."

"It wasn't always a poor place," Clara Tuck said sharply.

"Before Donovan?" Ruff guessed.

"That's right," Clara answered.

"Look, are you going to untie me sooner or later?" Ruff asked. "Because if you are, I'd appreciate having it done sooner."

"Yes. I'm sorry." She set the tray aside. She paused before she got to the knots.

Ruff told her in his most reassuring manner, "I won't attack you. I don't think I've got the strength anyway."

"It's just that . . . you must be angry."

"Untie me, Clara Tuck," Ruff said flatly, and she bobbed her head, obediently untying him.

The sensation shot back into his hands and feet. Annoying, sense-confusing needles and pins returned with the circulation. Ruff managed to reach over and scratch his nose with his left hand, and it seemed a great, satisfying accomplishment.

She sat back on the bed, small hands folded into her lap. "There."

"Why don't I sit up a little and eat, Clara Tuck. While I do that, tell me about this Mr. Donovan and Colly Higgins. All about Widow Creek and the days when this wasn't such a poor place."

She looked at him, noticed the amusement and concern in his eyes, the good humor playing on the lips of the broad mouth which lurked beneath that awful, drooping mustache, and she nodded.

"All right, I will." She picked up the tray apologetically. "It's mostly cold. I took a long time making up my mind to come in here. It's not easy to—"

"It's getting colder by the minute, Clara Tuck," Ruff said quietly, and she smiled, a little more deeply this time.

He took the tray and began eating. Ham, fried potatoes, corn. She had thoughtfully cut the meat. Ruff's chest still flooded with pain if he inadvertently moved that right arm. It would be a while before he had full use of that hand again.

He chewed the well-smoked ham and watched her, waiting. She glanced up nervously, shifting on the bed.

"I really shouldn't tell anyone el—"

Ruff frowned. He swallowed and coaxed her, "Come

on now, Clara, I'm not on their side and I'm obviously quite harmless anyway."

"All right," she agreed, although looking him up and down, she doubted that Ruff Justice was ever exactly harmless. "We settled up here twelve years ago. Bob and I, that is."

"Your husband?"

"Yes. He was. Dead now. That's how the creek got its name, you know. It's Widow Creek; I'm the widow. Before that it just had one of those wonderful but quite unpronounceable Indian names." She smiled, wistfully. "Bob purchased this land from the Arapaho. And that just wasn't done then. The Arapaho were very fierce and warlike twelve years back."

Ruff nodded. He remembered all too well. "But you got along with them?"

"Oh, well, very nearly. From time to time there was trouble. With the Arapahos and the Utes. Mostly it was horse stealing, things like that. We had a fine blooded herd of horses, you know. Bob sold them to the army mostly. It was a good life," she said with a sigh. Clara rose suddenly, walked in one tight circle, and then drew the rough wooden chair from the corner, watching Ruff chew his food for a minute.

"And then Donovan," he prompted.

"Yes." Her gray eyes turned suddenly as fierce as any Arapaho's. "That man came and he took it all away from us."

"What do you mean? How did he take it away from you?"

"A piece at a time, Mr. Justice. A bunch of horses, a bit of grass, a barn. And then finally he took Bob's life and there wasn't anything left of the place at all. Nothing but this house and a foolish woman."

"He wanted to run you off?"

"Yes. Absolutely, and he still does. But I won't leave,"

she said with gritty determination. "He can go to hell. I'll shoot him or any of his men I see on my property!" She blanched slightly, glancing at Ruff's wound. "That's about all of the story," she finished with a shrug.

"Except for the important part. Why? Why is he doing this? Is this land so valuable?"

"Not really. The grass isn't even that good. The spring is too short, you know. It was valuable while the horses were on the land."

"That's just my point. After the horses had been driven off, Donovan kept right on attacking your place. Does he want this land or does he simply want you off?"

"I really couldn't answer that."

"He never even told you?" Ruff asked incredulously. "You don't even know why?"

"No." She let her gray eyes settle on his. Her smile was empty, far away. "Isn't that something? It used to bother Bob tremendously. I can recall him sitting in this chair. Just sitting and repeating over and over, 'What does the man want? What?' He thought at first that it was an old enemy trying to get even with him."

"He had enemies?"

"Many of them." She paused. "He was a lawman, Mr. Justice. A territorial ranger, before he quit to buy this place. I am partly to blame, I suppose. I guess I nagged at Bob to give up his badge. It was terrible, never knowing when he would come back, if he would, you know? I thought that if we moved up here . . ." Her voice had grown husky, and Ruff knew she was on the verge of tears. They were tears she couldn't bear to shed in front of a stranger.

"I'm through eating," he said suddenly, and she nodded, stumbling to the bed. "We'll talk again," he said, and she nodded, keeping her face turned away from him. Quickly she picked up the tray and turned toward the door. And then she was gone, the room silent and empty, and smelling only faintly of her. She was a fine, proud woman, this Clara Tuck. She had guts and intelligence, and Ruff decided as he rolled over gingerly, the fading scent of her powder still lingering, that she was a damned fine-looking woman beneath the crust.

# 7.

....◆◆◆....

THE THUNDER RUMBLED heavily, rattling the window in Ruff's room. He opened his eyes to the darkness. The rain drummed down heavily. The leak at the foot of his bed had become a steady trickle. The roof needed to be resodded, and he wondered if anyone would ever do it.

Lightning glared on the window, and a moment later the heavy thunder sounded again as the rain, lashed by a driving wind, stuttered against the glass windowpanes.

Ruff was stiff, weary, and his back ached with the lying down. He decided to give standing up a try—another immobile hour in that bed seemed unendurable.

He moved slowly, swinging his feet toward the side of the bed, halting his motion if his chest protested too starkly. Finally he was sitting up, the blood rushing out of his head, leaving him dizzy, light-headed. After a minute, that cleared up and he tried putting his weight on his feet. Standing, he staggered only slightly, and he stood there in the dark room, his feet against the icy floor, feeling a complete man once again.

His chest was hot with pain. His head ached dully, but it was acceptable. He walked to the window, taking a slow deep breath, and small, cautious steps. The window was steamed over, and he rubbed a small circle clear with the heel of his hand.

Outside the land was a dark, furious hell. Dark rain falling over darker meadows. He could see the dead elm bending perilously before the wind, see the wind-flattened grass, and then suddenly, by the brilliant flash of nearby lightning, he saw Clara Tuck.

She was standing near the elm, at the corner of an old corral, but why? The wind was hard, the rain heavy as it slanted down. Yet she stood there placidly. The second flash of lightning, almost blinding in its blue-white intensity, revealed the reason.

A man sitting a rain-darkened horse, wearing a black slicker and tugged-down hat, was beside the corral, talking to Clara. The lightning blinked off, and Ruff could see no more of him.

He stood soberly watching the rain through the silvered window. Why on earth was she out there talking to the man? There could be only one reason for not coming into the house, into the warmth and out of the rain—the man didn't want to talk around Justice. What did that signify?

The dull headache had grown worse. Ruff turned away from the window. Just what sort of game was Clara Tuck playing? He thought suddenly of Sarah Kent and of one of Clara Tuck's exclamations—"I've been lied to by too many men."

Just then Ruff wondered if he hadn't been meeting too many lying women. Something was being hidden from him, and he didn't like the feeling. He could be leaving himself vulnerable. To what? He racked his brains. To Donovan or Colly Higgins, to James Kent, to the man in the rain . . .

He moved stiffly across the floor and stepped out into the cold main room. A few golden embers still burned beneath the gray ash in the fireplace, casting enough light to see by. Ruff passed the fireplace, and glancing occasionally at the door, he walked to the far corner, where he found what he was looking for. His saddle, saddlebags, rifle, and Colt.

He drew the pistol from its holster and opened the gate. The ammunition had been pulled. Squatting down—a motion which started his chest to protesting, his head throbbing—he slipped five .44s from the loops on his cartridge belt and loaded his pistol.

Then, with a last glance at the closed door, he walked back to his bed, feeling exhausted, cold, and puzzled. Deeply puzzled and more than a little wary. Slipping into bed, he laid the Colt beside his leg. After a minute Clara Tuck came back in, the draft of cold wind washing through the house as she opened the door.

She came stealthily to his door, peered in, and after a long minute, walked away. Justice lay there for a long while, listening to the night and the storm. Finally he slept, but it was not a deep sleep, and the fragmented brilliant dreams he had were filled with hostility and blood.

Morning dawned clear, and Ruff, stretching tenderly, awoke and slipped from the bed with only a little difficulty. He glanced at himself in the mirror, frowned at the bruised and unkempt face, and, thrusting the pistol behind his belt, he walked out into the living room.

Clara Tuck was busy over her stove, which was only a piece of plate steel set on a low brick support. She was muttering or singing in a very low voice, distracted by her work, and it was a moment before she sensed his presence. He saw her back go rigid, her head come up like a doe sensing a cougar, and then she spun, her eyes wide.

"Good morning," Justice said, and the terror fell away from her eyes.

"Don't ever do that!" She touched her breast with her fingertips. "My God! I thought it was Donovan. I didn't think you could move around yet."

"Not well. I did make it over to the window last night."

Her face gave nothing away, but she turned away rapidly, flipping her hotcakes over.

Ruff turned a chair and sat on it, facing the table,

watching her work with that busy concentration. "Who was it?" he asked.

"What?" She turned, smiling. "Who was what?"

"Last night. You met someone in the rain."

"Don't be silly." She laughed. She filled a plate with hotcakes and set it before Ruff.

He managed to cut them by using his fork and his left hand, and he ate slowly. Clara poured a cup of that terrible coffee and placed it before him apologetically. She sat at the table and began to eat, avoiding his eyes.

"Where's this Donovan holed up?" Ruff asked.

"What . . . ?" The question caught her in the midst of preoccupation. "Up on Cloud Peak. You just follow the creek three miles or so. His is the only place up there." She stopped abruptly. "Why do you want to know?"

"Just curious. I'm trying to understand your situation, Clara Tuck, but you're not helping me a whole lot."

"You don't need to understand it! It's none of your business, is it? I don't need any more help."

"Any more?" Ruff lifted an eyebrow.

"Do you want some coffee?" she asked, shifting her eyes away.

"No." He planted his elbows on the table and looked at her intently. "Look, Clara Tuck, I'm not a bad man. I just would like to know what your trouble is. Maybe I could help."

"More hotcakes?" she asked infuriatingly.

"Mind telling me what Donovan looks like?"

"Whatever for?"

"I'm just curious."

"He's fairly young," she said with a shrug. "Mid-thirties. Dark hair, mustache, blue eyes. Surly, tight little mouth."

Ruff nodded and bit at his lower lip. Finishing the coffee, he grimaced and put the cup aside. Clara was already busy washing the dishes in a wooden tub, her back turned firmly toward him. Ruff rose and went to his saddlebags, removing his shaving gear.

"Got a mirror hung somewhere?" he asked the woman.

"Outside by the outhouse," she said without turning her back. "Hung on the cottonwood tree."

He turned and shuffled toward the back door, passing near enough to taste the fragrance of her powder, to study the sturdy flair of her hips, the tough, straight back, the wisp of pale hair which fell along her sleek, sun-browned neck.

He opened the door and went out. The ground was thick with mud, the air clean, biting. A few clouds had assembled over the mountains to the west. A lone crow winged softly past.

The mirror, half-silvered, cracked, was tacked onto a cottonwood limb, and Ruff eyed himself in it. "Kinda battered up, old-timer," he told his reflection. He had his shaving cup and razor in hand. Looking around for water, he spotted with some surprise a pump near the corral. Bob Tuck hadn't been a rawhider—there probably wasn't another house with an indoor and an outdoor water pump for five hundred miles, unless it was Donovan's house.

Donovan. And how was it that his description came so near to answering that of James Kent? Ruff rinsed off at the pump and splashed some water into his shaving cup.

And there they were. The elm had kept enough of the rain off the tracks to leave them visible. Clara Tuck's small boots, and a perfectly defined set of larger boots.

"More lies, Clara Tuck?" he said under his breath. And why?

He had spent more time asking himself questions lately, and less time answering them. He walked back to the mirror and brushed up some lather. Soaping his face, he shaved, and as he did so he thought it out again.

Sarah Kent, missing. James Kent, missing. George Birch, missing. Kesselring dead. Clara Tuck frightened of a man named Donovan whose description would be a fair match for Kent's. Donovan wanted her off this place—or so she said. The woman lied, shot strangers, and met men in the dark and rain, making it difficult to trust her.

Ruff scraped his jaw, working carefully around the mustache, and rubbed his face vigorously with a towel. He ran his brush through his long, dark hair. Looking into the mirror again, he felt satisfied with the result.

He needed a new shirt. Standing there in the open with only a bandage to keep him warm, he wondered if any of Bob Tuck's clothing was still around.

He turned and started back toward the house, and his eyes lifted to the bulky, shadowed mountains beyond the valley. Three miles up along Widow Creek, she had said. That was where Ruff meant to go as soon as the wound allowed. He wanted very badly to visit this Mr. Donovan.

Clara Tuck was standing on the back porch, watching his approach as he returned to the house. Her expression was tight, unpleasant. He knew he wasn't wanted, and that had to be what was going through her mind.

"You shouldn't have shot me," he said, stepping onto the porch.

"Or I should have shot you better."

"Now, Clara, I thought we were past that stage," he chided gently.

"Yes." She smiled slowly, her gray eyes meeting his briefly. "I guess we are past that."

She was a complex woman, a worried woman. All of that showed in her eyes, in her small, nearly furtive gestures. And there was no way of helping her, apparently, none at all.

"I thought you might still have some of your husband's shirts somewhere," Ruff said as they reentered the living room.

She turned toward him as if he had struck her, her fists bunched, her face lined with emotion, but gradually she relaxed. "Yes," she said hurriedly, "of course." She looked at his wound, his bare shoulders, and then scurried from the room. "I'm afraid there's nothing long enough," her voice said from deep within the bedroom. He heard her rummaging in a closet. "There's this," she said to herself.

After a minute she came back bearing a maroon shirt at arm's length.

It had embossed silver buttons and looked as if it had never been worn. Clara Tuck's eyes were misted over with memory. Maybe a shirt that didn't fit, a birthday present he didn't like. One of those thousands of small memories married couples accumulate had come back vividly to haunt her briefly.

"That'll do fine," Ruff said, taking it from her. "Think you could help me into it? My right arm doesn't go too good."

He smiled and she nodded, helping him shoulder into the shirt, which was a bit too large in the chest, a little short in the sleeves. Ruff turned the cuffs up once and nodded. "Just fine. I'm sorry, Clara Tuck, but I need a shirt."

"It's all right. It's just—I still have little twinges. Seeing you in that shirt now . . . it's difficult still."

After stowing his gear, Ruff took a chair out onto the front porch and sat there in the sun, feet propped up on the rail, watching the quicksilver creek, the deep-purple mountains, the activity of the birds and animals in the forest, the wind bending the lush long grass, and he decided that Bob Tuck had been a lucky man for a time. A very lucky man.

He lazed away most of the day, dozing and daydreaming. It was already nearly sundown when the squeaking of a porch plank caused his eyelids to flicker open.

Clara Tuck had come out onto the porch. The late sunlight caught her golden hair and defined the planes of her face. The wind toyed with the light cotton dress she wore.

She stood leaning against the porch railing, lost in her own thoughts.

Ruff's voice was low, faint:

> "The river runs with bright emotion
> Sweeping mountains to the sea
> Yet I must never see that ocean.
> I stand and watch it flow away
> Still anchored to your memory."

"What's that?" she asked. Her face turned to his, and she noticed for the first time a deep quiet in the man's blue eyes.

"Nothing. Something I wrote for someone long, long ago."

"Someone who went away?"

"Someone who was taken away by time," he replied.

She turned, leaning against the porch railing. "You wrote it? I think it's very beautiful."

"Do you? Thanks. You're kinder than some people have been. My poetry is . . ." He paused. "Sincere."

"But it's very good!"

"That is where folks tend to differ," Ruff admitted, his grin returning. For a minute there it had been difficult. The poem, as it always did, recalled Four Dove in that faraway mountain retreat. It wasn't good, perhaps, as poetry. But it brought her to life to recite it. Maybe, in that way, Clara Tuck understood it.

"Recite some more, will you?" she asked.

"More? All right, but not that sort of stuff. There's one I wrote about the hanging of a gambler named Bill Towers—it was a favorite of Wild Bill Hickok's."

"All right," she agreed tentatively. How grisly, she thought, but when Justice recited it she was captivated. Bill Towers had been hung by mistake, but he had apparently had such a sordid background that it was justice in its own way.

She alternately smiled and frowned, her nose drawing

down as her eyes squinted with enjoyment. He leaned back in his chair, waving his arms, losing himself in the rhythm of the poem, and she wondered, wondered just what sort of man this was.

When he was through she found that she liked him more. Why, how, she could not be sure. She urged him on.

"If you don't mind," he agreed. "Usually at about this point I have to hold my six-gun in my lap to keep folks from bolting toward the door." He grinned again, and she smiled deeply in return. "I recall Zebulon Pike," he said by way of introduction, and he launched into another epic:

"He came when the prairie was young
Unscarred by wagon-wheel ruts
When the flowers lay like carpets of gold
And crimson and blue across the plains
And the only music was the song the wind sung."

She listened and found that she was listening with other senses than her ears. She watched him, tall and lean, dressed in her husband's shirt, his expressive hands gesturing, his mouth at once mournful and careless, his deep-blue eyes meeting hers with sudden emphasis, and she felt a chill creep up her spine.

And then he was finished, the words trailing away, seeming somehow to linger on his lips, and she wondered about the man. She wondered.

Ruff looked to the mountains, deep in shadow already. Dusk came early here, and with dusk the wind rose. Flat, leaden clouds crept in from the northwest. It was likely it would rain again.

"You'll catch a chill out here," Clara told him, and he nodded.

"You're right." He stood, stumbled slightly, and felt the weight of Clara Tuck against him, supporting him. "Damn leg. I'm sorry."

"It's not your fault. It's your wound." She was looking up at him now with those gray eyes, and they seemed at once childish and cunning. Justice was in no danger of falling now, but she made no move to draw away from him. She stood, shoulder under his arm, her hand at the small of his back, her eyes dazed.

"Let's go in," he said quietly, and she nodded.

He led her into the house, still clinging to her, and as they entered the living room she closed the door behind them and drew in the latch string.

# 8.

••••———◆———••••

RUFF LAY ON the bed, the sheet drawn up over him. The last light through the window glossed Clara Tuck's golden hair and danced in her eyes as she undressed before him nervously.

"I never did this with anyone but my husband."

He nodded and said, "You don't have to do it now."

"No, I know I don't," she said. Her hands, behind her back, had finished the row of buttons, and she slid the gingham dress from her shoulders. The skin she revealed was pale, smooth, flawless. She smiled uneasily, keeping her eyes from Ruff's.

She sat to tug off her boots, and Ruff's eyes stayed on her in pleasurable anticipation. He studied the long, lithe arms of the woman, the shape of her neck, the small, dextrous hands.

She looked appealing sitting there in that ribboned chemise, appealing and quite sensuous. Slowly she lifted her hands to her hair, and she unpinned it. It was much longer than Ruff had thought; it fell in waves the color of cornsilk across her shoulders.

She smiled, took courage, and stood, undoing her chemise. When she stepped from it she was naked, lovely in the last pale light. She had firm, shapely breasts with prominent nipples, flaring, purposeful hips, straight, smooth legs. A golden patch of soft down between her thighs riveted his interest, and even in the dim light he could see her blush.

She rushed across the cold floor to the bed, and he noticed now that her eyes were no longer shy. They seemed aroused, electric. She leaned to him and gave him a kiss which was far from tentative. Her lips were supple, active. Her hair fell across his chest, brushed his cheek.

"Well, now," she said, sitting beside him, *"you've* seen *me."* She drew the sheet down, and he could see that she was pleased as her eyes swept down across his abdomen to his crotch, where his growing need must have been obvious. "Oh, my," she breathed as if startled, but there was pleasure in the exclamation as well.

"You can't move around very much, can you?" She brushed her hair back from her face. "Well, then, I suppose it's up to me."

Ruff lay back, his eyes drinking in the contours of her body, which was nearly a silhouette now as darkness settled. Thunder rumbled in the distance, and he hoped the roof didn't start leaking at the wrong time in the wrong place.

He saw her arch her back, stretch out a hand, and he felt the examination of soft fingers. His erection was hefted, tested, inflamed. She closed her hand, which was barely able to encircle him, and with a tiny shudder she began to stroke him. Her movements were gentle, almost shy, but her excitement was unmistakable.

The bed trembled slightly; he heard her soft, agitated breathing. His hand stretched out slowly and touched the smooth, inner contour of her silky thigh. She stiffened automatically, and then relaxed. Ruff's hand swept across her thigh slowly until she began to silently urge him on. Her pelvis was thrust toward him, and he felt the brush of downy hair against his fingertips.

Exploring upward, he found damp, soft flesh, warm and slick with eagerness, and he slipped his fingers inside her, bringing a shudder to her thighs. Her hand tightened on his cock in response.

Slowly they touched each other, fondling eager, swollen flesh, their breathing becoming more rapid, more intent, until Clara broke away from him and eased onto his abdomen, facing away from him so that he could rest his hands on the white half-globes of her fantastically smooth, amazingly strong buttocks.

She stretched out so that her hands rested on his ankles. Her buttocks tilted upward and away from him, and Ruff's hands met at her crotch. His fingers traced smooth ellipses around her flesh. The obvious, increasing dampness of her inflamed him. He sought and found the tiny, rigid tab of flesh there and toyed with it slowly until Clara, her hips beginning to thrust and roll, could stand it no longer.

Then her hand brushed his as she clutched at his crotch, finding his swollen, ready erection, and she fitted him to her, settling on him with a shudder as he slid deeply inside. He let his hands rest on her buttocks, and watched as she sat with her neck arched, her arms rigid against his thighs. She made a small, unintelligible sound, and he heard the grating of her teeth as she trembled against him, felt the working of the muscles inside of her warm sheath of flesh.

She had been holding her breath, it seemed. Now it burst from her explosively, and she began to pant as she swayed, each expulsion of breath accompanied by a small, mewing sound. He could no longer see her in the darkness. He could only feel her. Her catlike movements, the pagan rhythm of her, the warmth of flesh, the tensing and relaxing of thigh muscles.

She swayed and pitched against him. Her hands clutched wildly at his legs as she worked deliberately, occasionally uttering a small sound which reflected her deep concentration, the sound of a body at its work.

The slow, steady pulsing gave way suddenly to a mad

rush toward completion. She had been long without a man, and this was an act of forgetting, an act which was to obliterate all of her troubles, her loneliness, and then it was something else. It was a wild, writhing feast. She devoured him, clutched at his legs, his cock, her back straight as a yardstick, her hips fluid as a panther's, as she tried to drive him more deeply into her.

Ruff felt her inner muscles slacken, tighten, go slack again; he felt the damp flow within her, felt her hands clawing at him. His own hands held fast to her writhing hips and he tried to draw her down still farther, to bury himself in her.

She scooted against him, her breath coming in hot, jerky gasps, and then with a grinding thrust of her pelvis against his she stopped abruptly. Stopped and made a small sound not unlike the chirp of a bird. Stopped for only a moment and then began swaying methodically against him, and Ruff knew that he couldn't hold back any longer.

He thrust up with his hips, gripping her buttocks so tightly that it must have hurt her, but she was lost in her dreamy swaying, her hands kneading his thighs like a cat's paws.

He thrust against her, and she swayed from side to side tantalizingly, her flesh warm, eager against his, and the slow thudding which had been building in Ruff's loins turned into a demanding torrent which he could no more hold back than a man can hold back the sea.

He drove into her, gripping her tightly, feeling her strong, eager response, hearing her small sounds of pleasure, her scent filling his nostrils, and he reached a hard, deeply satisfying climax, holding her against him as her body continued to quiver, to ripple with waves of excitement which slowly settled to exhaustion.

Side by side they lay on the bed, her light fingertips running across his chest, his hip, her lips brushing his shoulder, throat, and mouth.

The rain had begun, and the roof was leaking, but it couldn't have mattered less.

Thunder boomed close at hand and then boomed again. The third time it was not thunder at all. A bullet smashed through the window of the bedroom, spraying shards of glass.

Ruff rolled from the bed, tearing open his chest, and he cursed with the pain. Rifle fire peppered the house. From the kitchen he could hear the smashing of dishes, the ricochet of bullets off an iron pot. The window in the main room was shattered by a hail of bullets.

Ruff had his Colt in his hand, and he crept toward the door. The door was punched full of bullet holes, and as he reached it another volley of shots slammed into it.

He pressed back against the wall as splinters flew from door and frame, as another blast—this time from a shotgun—riddled the window, spraying the room with wood and glass.

He edged toward the window, saw the blur of a man on horseback through the rain, and fired. The shot brought an answering fusillade of lead, and he crouched, spinning away from the window, as the bullets slammed into the walls of the house.

He was suddenly aware of the faint scent of smoke, and looking toward the back of the house he saw flames leaping up, bright orange and golden, curling against the dark, rainy night skies.

There was one last shot and then the drumming of horses' hoofs as the nightriders rode away from the ranch house. Ruff leaped to the window and emptied his Colt after them, probably futilely, but there was a rage in him, a rage against men who would swoop down on a widow's house in the dead of night and do this.

The flames were still burning brightly at the back of the house, and Ruff, naked in the cold night, went outside, kicking open the shattered back door.

The flames were sputtering in the rain, but they had a

good hold on the eaves. Looking around, Ruff found an ax by the woodpile, and with that he began to battle the fire. It was hazardous, dressed as he was. Several times falling debris threatened to burn him in uncomfortable places. Yet he stretched out and hacked at the eaves, cutting the charred and burning wood away from the rest of the house.

How much good he did, he couldn't say. The rain had increased, and driving down, it smothered the fire, leaving only cold smoke to wisp up against the night. Ruff stood watching the roof for a time, making sure it didn't catch fire again. It was damned cold. The rain drove against his back. His legs shivered, and he knew he had torn his chest open with that work.

He found a cold torch on the ground. A torch cast onto the roof by one of the nightriders. And if it hadn't been raining? A woman burned to death or burned out of her home, left with nothing in the world.

They had killed her husband, driven off her horses, and now they would even take away her home. A bullet might easily have taken her life. Ruff felt a cold, sullen anger building inside of him. It was not what he had come to Widow Creek to do, but this night had decided him—Donovan, whoever the bastard was, would pay for this. He would pay in full.

Shivering, Ruff went back through the rain toward the door, stepping over the still-smoldering debris. He passed through the doorway where a useless, birdshot-riddled door hung aslant.

He crossed the dark, cold rooms and returned to the bedroom. It was a time before he could see her, but he heard her clearly enough.

A small, childlike cry, the deep, helpless sobbing of a woman utterly defeated, filled the room. He found her wrapped in a sheet, huddled in the corner of the room, and as he sat down beside her and touched her shoulder, she recoiled with fear.

Then she turned, eyes wide, recognized him, and threw her arms around him, holding on to him with all of her might, clinging to him, this one feeble hope.

"They couldn't even let me have one night, one moment of happiness," she said, her voice muffled as she pressed her face against his shoulder. "Not even that much!"

"It won't happen again," Ruff said. He held her tightly, rocking her like a child. "I swear this will not happen again!"

He sat beside her in the darkness for a long while until her sobbing slowed and finally ceased. He sat there, her heavy head against his chest, listening to the rain and the wind sounds, the scent of the woman and of cold, damp ashes in his nostrils.

And then there was another sound. Clara Tuck's head came up. Her eyes were wide, and she wagged her head from side to side in panic.

Ruff walked to the bed, slipped into his pants, and stood in the deep shadows, listening. What was that?

He placed it now—near the front door. A scratching as if an animal were at the house, a dog trying to get in by the hearth, a bear testing the strength of the hinges.

Clara cowered in the corner, and Ruff slipped out, crossing the room on tiptoes. Beside the door he halted, stilling his breath, listening for the sound. But it didn't come again.

There was nothing but the rain and the shrill cry of the gusting wind. Holding his Colt beside his ear, Ruff stepped to the door, cautiously and slowly lifting the bar from its brackets.

That done, he held the door to with his toe as he set the bar to one side against the wall.

He drew his thumb back, and the ratcheting sound of the big Colt being cocked seemed loud in the stillness. He steadied himself, took a deep breath, gripped the edge of the door, and pulled it open, lowering his pistol simultaneously.

Clara shrieked behind him, and he glanced across his shoulder to see her standing in the bedroom doorway, the sheet around her shoulders, her fingertips to her mouth.

Ruff turned back to the open door. He shoved the pistol behind his waistband and crouched low over the man who lay there.

The rain drove down; the trees trembled in the night wind, and the man on the porch lay shirtless, badly wounded or dead, his fingers raw and bloody from clawing at the door.

"Oh, Jesus!" Clara said in what was more prayer than curse. "Is it . . . who is it?"

Ruff dragged him inside, replaced the bar in its brackets, and lit a lantern, already knowing who it was, already knowing he would not survive.

Ruff returned to the injured man and squatted on his heels. Someone had tied a rope around him and dragged him for miles. His body was a mass of bruises and lacerations. His arm was obviously broken, and those deep feverish eyes were flooded with incomprehensible pain. It was George Birch.

"I'm dying," he muttered through split lips. His eyes wavered and finally focused on Clara Tuck. "Sorry, Clara. I'm afraid I've let you down. It didn't work."

"Get some soap and water, bandages. Carbolic if you've got it," Ruff told her, and she scurried away.

"It's too late," Birch said. "I'm all busted up inside."

"You'll make it," Ruff lied.

"Sure." He smiled weakly and choked, coughing up a dab of scarlet blood. Suddenly he gripped Ruff's arm tightly and lifted his head. "Help her, will you? I'm sorry. I couldn't talk to you about any of it. I didn't know who the hell you were. . . . Help her."

"Sure," Ruff answered. "Don't worry about that."

Birch's grip loosened on his sleeve. His head lolled

back on a neck which couldn't support it. Ruff eased the man as much as possible. Rolling up Clara's slicker, he placed it under Birch's head for a pillow. He didn't dare move Birch, not knowing what was broken up inside, and so Birch lay against the cold floor, his teeth chattering, his eyes feverish.

"I didn't take time to heat the water," Clara said, handing him the basin.

"That's all right," he assured her. It would make no difference—nothing would make any difference to Birch. He wished the man would hold on for long enough to explain all of this, but even that seemed unlikely.

Ruff got to work, trying to clean up the terrible wounds on George Birch's body. His chest was scabbed with mud and blood. Cleaning that away, Ruff found something that made him wince.

"Oh!" Clara had returned with a blue bottle filled with carbolic, and by the feeble lanternlight she too saw the mutilation.

They had taken a knife and cut a star into his chest, going deep, as savage as any Indian. Ruff cleaned the wound with soap and water and then applied the acrid carbolic. "What's that about?" he asked Clara.

"He . . . he was a lawman, Ruff. He *is* a lawman," she corrected. But she too was already thinking of George Birch as a dead man. "He knew my husband."

Ruff shook his head. Birch was out of his mind. Clara had covered him with a blanket, but there was a chill seeping into George Birch's body, a chill which no amount of warmth could drive away.

He lay with his eyes closed, occasionally murmuring something neither of them could understand. His head rolled from side to side in anguish, and his face had taken on a gray pallor. Finally his writhing slowed and ceased. He lay still as death, but his chest rose and fell faintly. Abruptly those eyes flickered open as if he had been yanked back from the gates. "Donovan . . . Kent," he said, his eyes coming into sharp focus.

"I know," Ruff told him. "Don't worry. I'll get him."

"Donovan . . . Kent," he repeated, but his voice was slurred, his jaw slack. And then he said no more. He lay there, cold, inert against the cabin floor.

Clara let out a little moan and sagged into a chair, burying her face in her hands. "I'll bury him," Ruff said, rising.

"Now?"

"Now." What was there to wait for? Clara would be better off once he was out of sight. Ruff took a minute to rifle his clothing, hoping to find something of use, but there was nothing at all. Someone had evidently already gone through his pockets.

Standing, Ruff opened the door and peered out. Dark as death with rain hammering down, the drops rebounding a foot off the hard-packed yard. He returned, crouched low, and gathered up what had been George Birch.

He buried him near the elm, working slowly in the cold, driving rain, the night winds chilling him. He rolled Birch into the trench and covered him with the sodden earth. He stood over the grave for a minute, the rain washing his hair across his face, feeling as he always did in the presence of the dead, a little less alive himself, futile and vaguely ashamed.

Then he turned and walked back to the house where a lonely, broken woman waited.

"Use this," she said, handing him a heavy towel, and Ruff nodded his thanks. Stripping down, he rubbed himself from head to toe, reviving the circulation. Then, the towel around him, he sat near the fire which Clara had started. She had made coffee for them. Dark, bitter coffee. The ear of Ruff's mug was missing. Almost everything in the kitchen had been damaged by gunfire.

The flames flickered, spun arabesques, and slowly

spread a gentle warmth through the room. Clara sat beside him in silent thought, and Ruff let her have her reflective moment before he said, "Tell me about it now."

"No." Her face was an emotionless mask, her voice low. "I don't want you to do anything. I don't want anyone else to die."

"I understand that, Clara. But believe this—I'm going ahead anyway. I'm going to see Mr. Donovan and speak to him in a language he will understand."

"No—that's what George tried to do!"

"I'm not George."

"I won't have you die on my account."

"Clara, that's something which happens to be my choice, not yours. I'm going after the man. Now, you can help me maybe, by telling me what you know. But you can't change my mind by not telling me about it."

She looked up, her face pretty, youthful in the golden firelight. Her hair framed her face with soft spun gold. Her eyes were distant, troubled. A hand reached out and rested on Ruff's own.

"Don't you see . . . I can't have you die too."

"I'll do my best not to," he said, and she just shook her head, not understanding this at all. How could he smile?

"Oh, Justice, damn!" she breathed. Clara touched her hair and leaned back in her chair. Firelight cast wavering shadows in the hollows of her cheeks. "I'll tell you what I know," she said finally.

A log burned through and sagged in the fireplace. The wind funneled down the chimney and whipped the flames. Sarah composed herself and leaned back in the rocker. She told him what she knew, as little as it was.

"Bob and George Birch went back a long way. They were district marshals together in Denver. After Bob dropped out of law enforcement he still kept in touch with George. One summer George spent a week here, fishing, hunting in the mountains . . . it was a fine summer." Her eyes glazed over with reminiscence.

"I believe Bob asked George to look into Donovan's past when this trouble first started, but I'm not sure. Anyway, when Bob"—she took a deep breath and managed to say it—"was murdered, I wrote to George and told him about it. I told him that this man Donovan was almost certainly responsible for it, and I asked him for help."

"Where was Birch then?"

"The United States Marshal's office in Washington."

"He would have had access to a lot of information of different sorts," Ruff commented. Birch could very well have seen the army report on James Kent if he had somehow managed to trace Donovan back to Kent. It was possible, too, especially if he had been working on it for some time as Clara suspected. Then what? An inquiry into close relatives, a decision to follow Sarah Kent. The odds were that General Hightower's information had the same source as that Birch had contacted.

"George came through here before you arrived, Ruff, and he told me he had fallen in with the Donovan gang, that he was accumulating evidence. In the meantime, he warned me to keep the door barred and my rifle at hand. He said that from what he had heard at the Donovan ranch they were far from through with me."

"Did he say why they wanted you off this property?" Ruff asked.

"No. All he knew was that they did." She glanced up. "He also warned me that a tall man in buckskins was following him. He thought you were probably a Donovan man sent to escort Sarah—was that her name?—to the ranch."

"I suppose he would think that." After all, he and Sarah Kent had acted like old friends. Or more. Ruff kept his expression bland. It seemed Clara was probing a little.

No wonder Birch had tried to dump him. At the first opportunity he had hired Kesselring, a known man, and hit the plains. But he had begun to think it was Birch who had thrown him overboard back on the river. But Birch was a marshal, and he didn't think they resorted to those tactics. Was it after all only the outraged card cheat, Updike? Clara went on.

"George managed to sneak away from the ranch—the night you saw him talking to me out in the rain. He told me he was ready to arrest Donovan and break up that gang, but he felt there was a joker in the deck." Ruff's eyebrows raised.

"A joker? What did he mean?"

"I have no idea. I told him about you and he warned me not to say anything. He said it could cost him his life. . . . Well," she said, closing her eyes, "it looks like it didn't matter."

Ruff was silent. Birch had made a mistake somewhere. It had cost him his life. They had discovered he was a lawman. The star cut into his chest was meant as a warning—to Ruff? How could they even know Justice was in that house? Perhaps it was only meant to shake up Clara, to warn her not to try calling in the law again. In that, it had worked.

The woman was beaten, empty, dry. At least that was what Ruff thought until she spoke, her low voice barely audible above the crackling of the fire.

"They'll have to kill me too." She lifted her eyes to Ruff—very lovely gray eyes with flecks of gold in them, just now, very somber eyes. "They want me to go away. They've threatened, burned, killed. But I won't go. You see, Ruff, I don't have any place to go. I haven't got folks back East, haven't got friends. All I ever had was Bob and this place. So I can't go—there's nowhere to go. That's where their calculations have gone wrong."

Ruff stood and walked behind her chair. Resting his hands on her shoulders, he kissed her hair once, gently. Then, in silence, they watched the fire burn to dully glowing embers as the house went cold, as the storm outside raged on.

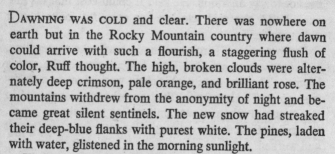

# 9.

Dawning was cold and clear. There was nowhere on earth but in the Rocky Mountain country where dawn could arrive with such a flourish, a staggering flush of color, Ruff thought. The high, broken clouds were alternately deep crimson, pale orange, and brilliant rose. The mountains withdrew from the anonymity of night and became great silent sentinels. The new snow had streaked their deep-blue flanks with purest white. The pines, laden with water, glistened in the morning sunlight.

The frosted grass beneath the hoofs of Justice's horse was dazzling in the sunlight. Each drop of moisture became jewel-like, glittering red and purple, green as the blue roan tracked across the broad valley.

A herd of grazing elk lifted wary heads and froze, like a brilliantly executed tapestry. Deep-violet shadows filled the canyons where racing freshets ran down water-polished chutes.

Farther down, tenacious wildflowers clung to their brief moment in the sun. Scarlet trumpet, blue gentian, fields of black-eyed susans stretching out endlessly over untrampled grasslands.

Ruff took it all in, the vivid color, the subtle patterns of shadow beneath the trees, the towering, slope-sided high mountains, and he cursed Donovan. Cursed him for cutting a man off who loved this land. A man who had braved the hard winters, the Indians, the hostile land, to live among beauty. He cursed the man Donovan for having taken Bob Tuck away from all he loved, for having left that pale, silent woman alone in that half-burned house along Widow Creek.

She had watched him with silent, resigned eyes as he saddled the blue roan and accepted the sack of supplies from her hand. She had watched as he turned westward, toward Cloud Peak and Donovan's ranch.

Watched and then turned away, so that he would not see the hot tears in her eyes. But he had seen them, and there had been nothing to say. Not even "Don't worry, I won't die." That was always a foolish boast.

He had gone a mile toward Cloud Peak when he saw the dust rising from the mass of pines above and to the west. Ruff drew his horse aside, walking it into the trees beside the road, and he waited in the shadows.

After half an hour they came into sight. Six very tough-looking men, each leading a spare horse. Ruff pressed his back up against a large pine, merging with the shadowed trees, gripping his rifle tightly.

They came so near that he could make out their faces. Their leader seemed to be a huge Mexican with a handlebar mustache. He laughed out loud as they neared Ruff's hiding place.

". . . for Sonora, myself."

"I never . . . better myself," a lanky redheaded kid answered.

"You wait and see," another rider answered, his voice fading out as they rounded a bend in the trail. ". . . all be rich after . . ."

And then they were gone. Ruff listened to the dying sounds of their horses, wondering if those were the very men who had raided the house on Widow Creek the night before. There was no telling. One thing was certain— these were not ordinary cowhands. And, Clara had told him, there was no one up on Cloud Peak but Donovan and his gang.

Ruff rode his horse through the timber, and at the top of the hill he watched until the band of men had taken the right-hand fork of the road, up the nameless canyon to the south. They were not heading for Widow Creek, but where? From the look of them they were planning on a long hard ride.

Yet that might make it easier for Ruff. Six men away from the mountain meant six fewer adversaries—how many more did Donovan have up there?

There was no answering that, and Ruff turned his horse westward once more. Back on the trail he moved more cautiously. There was an abundance of fresh tracks on that road. Cattle, horses, and wagons had passed this way in numbers. The rain must have washed away most of the older sign—this was all recent.

Ruff drew up suddenly, understanding. There was one reason why Donovan wanted Clara Tuck out of Widow Creek, and only one. There was too much she could see there. Cattle being driven to Cloud Peak. Whose cattle? Horses. Again, whose? There was too damned much activity up and down this road, probably related to activity best kept hidden.

She was in the way. Clara Tuck threatened Donovan simply by being a witness to all of this activity. Donovan was the sort who would not want witnesses.

He rode through the trees into the afternoon, avoiding the road, which was evidently well traveled, and when the shadows had already grown long, when the wind flowing down from off the mountains had increased and grown chill, he came upon the ranch.

From the wind-flooded hillrise where the great pines creaked and swayed in the wind, Ruff could see into the mountain valley where a white house, three roughly constructed outbuildings, and a corral stood.

There were half a hundred horses visible, and probably

five times that number up in the isolated valleys above the house. Smoke rose from the stone chimney of the low white house itself and from one of the outbuildings, probably a bunkhouse.

A flash of color against the prevailing blue-green of the forest drew Ruff's eye to an outrider who was slowly circling the meadow, keeping to the forest himself. The man wore a buffalo coat and a hat with a red-and-yellow band. Searching more carefully, Ruff was able to pick out another man across the valley. How many were there unseen?

He slipped from the blue roan's back, loosened the cinches, and squatted on his heels, studying the layout of the ranch.

A man in a white apron appeared on the sagging porch of what Ruff took to be the bunkhouse. He was carrying a pan of water, and now he tossed it out onto the ground. Looking around, the man rolled a smoke and perched on the porch railing, puffing at it.

It was already growing dark in the narrow valley. Dusk colored the grass to purple. The cook rose, threw away his smoke, and clanged away on a triangle hung from the awning.

Suppertime. It wasn't long before the hands started for the bunkhouse, and Ruff counted seven men. The outriders stayed where they were, riding in slow circles. Donovan wanted no one arriving unannounced.

In the gathering shadows, Ruff thought it over. True, he might be able to breach Donovan's security and sneak up on the house, with a lot of luck. And then what? If the man Donovan resembled Kent, whom Justice had never seen, snatch him and try to sneak back through the guards, returning the suspect to the Indian Nation?

It didn't make a whole lot of sense.

Nor did the only alternative. Ride in there bold as brass, find Sarah Kent, and determine in that way if Donovan was her brother? And then . . . the plan sort of faltered at that point.

"Just what the hell else is there to do?" he asked the horse, which pricked its ears curiously but made no reply.

Kent or Donovan had never seen Ruff. A point in his favor. They couldn't know he had spoken to Clara Tuck. They shouldn't know that he was working for the army. Although there had been the attack by Colly Higgins and his men in Kit Carson—a definite warning.

Ruff decided suddenly to go ahead and brass it out. Donovan must be a suspicious man, but he couldn't believe that another lawman would follow so closely on the heels of George Birch. At least Ruff hoped not. What Birch had gotten had been a hell of a lot more than a warning.

"All right," he said, rising. "We'll try it." The horse had no opinion. Ruff dusted the pine needles from his pants and tightened the cinches.

Swinging into the saddle, he returned to the road and headed toward the Donovan Ranch, singing as he rode.

> *"They hung Billy Birch to a white oak tree*
> *They left him to dry in the sun*
> *And killin' his wife and mother-in-law*
> *Was all that poor Billy had done. . . ."*

"Hold up there." The voice was low, authoritative, and accompanied by a scattergun.

"Evenin'," Ruff said amiably. He leaned on the saddle-horn, watching the guard slowly emerge from the pines, his eyes going down Ruff's backtrail.

"Why don't you just turn around, partner," the guard suggested. "You've got the wrong trail."

"Not at all," Justice answered lightly. He did notice that the hammers on that shotgun were drawn back. "I'm lookin' for a party named Kent. Friend of mine. Said if I was ever in the neighborhood—"

"You got the wrong place," the guard said. But Ruff

had seen his eyebrows rise, his forehead furrow as the name Kent was dropped.

"Listen, I know y'all got to be cautious," Ruff went on. "But I'm tellin' you it's all right. I'm an old friend." As he spoke, Ruff measured the lean, dark man facing him, calculated his chances of beating that scattergun if it came to that, and liked none of his answers.

"What's going on, Ed?"

A second rider, summoned by their voices, appeared.

"Man wants to come on in."

"Sorry. This is a private road," the newcomer said.

"Yeah," Ruff said casually, "your pal told me that, but—"

"Says he knows someone named Kent," Ed told his partner. They exchanged glances, and the other man shrugged.

"Have to let the boss decide, I guess," he said. But he turned to Ruff. "If you're lying, partner, you're liable to regret this day the rest of your short life."

"Y'all are raisin' too much of a fuss," Ruff said. He leaned forward across the roan's withers and winked. "I don't blame you for bein' careful, but y'all are overdoin' it."

"I'll have to take your guns," Ed said, and Ruff handed them over cheerfully.

"Hope I haven't missed grub," Ruff said. "How is it here, anyway?"

No one answered. The two guards traded glances again, and he hoped that they weren't planning on just taking him off into the woods and blowing some ventilation through him.

But if Ruff was guessing right, that would be "the boss's" decision. How he would handle that was another matter. Kent had already killed a U.S. marshal, he wasn't likely to balk at having a drifter executed.

They rode across the dark meadow, and Ed whistled

loudly twice, and was answered from the roof of the main house.

Ruff sat his horse with Ed beside him while the other man tramped across the porch of the house and almost apologetically knocked.

The door swung open, and a blaze of light stung Ruff's eyes. Damned if that house wasn't hung with chandeliers! And by their light he could see red velvet furniture, paneled walls, and parquet flooring. All astonishing in a house which from the outside appeared to be a modest ranch house.

The man who answered the door was dressed as a butler, but he had a sullen scowl and a scar running across from his eye to his chin. The men muttered together, and the door was closed.

"Get down," Ed told Ruff, and Justice slid from the horse, swinging his long leg up and over the horse's neck.

Together the three of them stood in the shadows cast by the lights from within, and Ruff heard the distinctive, haunting sound of a harmonica drifting across the meadow from the bunkhouse or near it.

The door opened again and the cutthroat butler waved them in. With a guard on either side, Ruff stepped up onto the porch and through the wide oak door. He was guided down a long carpeted hallway, and they halted next to a second door. The butler went in alone.

Ed leaned a shoulder against the wall and regarded Ruff with open curiosity and some amusement. The door opened, and the two guards fell back as Ruff Justice, hat in hands, walked into the formal dining room.

A sleek, dark-haired man sat at the head of the table, which was lighted by two candelabras, spread with linen and set with crystal and silver.

The man looked up from his plate, fork couched in his sun-browned hand, and said quietly, "I never saw him before in my life. Get rid of him."

"Yes, sir, Mr. Donovan."

Hands gripped Ruff's arms tightly, and Ed said mockingly, "Goddamn liar." He managed to smile while he said it, and Ruff found himself taking a dislike to Ed.

"Now hold it." Justice tried to shrug off the hands which held him, but they were stuck good. He offered his best "aw-shucks" smile to the man at the head of the table and said, "I never saw this·fella before, either. Never said I did."

"Well, damn you, if you didn't . . . !" Ed sputtered.

"I said I was looking for a friend named Kent," Ruff reminded them. "And if I'm not almighty wrong . . ." He looked at the woman in white satin who had half risen from her chair, an expression of mingled pleasure and astonishment on her face. Her lips were frozen in disbelief; her dark-blue eyes smiled at him.

"Ruffin T. Justice," Sarah said by way of welcome. She put her napkin aside and stepped around the end of the table. The man at the table's head was frowning deeply.

"Hello, Sarah. Lord, it's good to see you. Thought I'd lost you for good and all."

"Who is this, Sarah?" the man asked peevishly.

"It's Mr. Justice, a friend of mine. My guide. You recall me telling you about the tall man. This is the one."

Now the man rose, slapping his napkin down. He nodded, and the hands fell away from Ruff's arms though the guards didn't withdraw.

"You must be James Kent," Ruff said, thrusting out a hand. "Your sister's told me all about you."

Kent went stiff as a board. The vein across his forehead grew prominent, and his eyes went cold as sin.

"How are you, Mr. Justice?" he said, managing to keep his voice calm. "Have you eaten? Join us. Andrew, another place, if you please."

The scarred butler bowed from the neck and turned toward an inner door. Kent had the outward grace of a man caught in an awkward social situation, but his anger wasn't far beneath the surface. His eyes, glittering with malice, flickered from Sarah to Justice and back again.

They sat at the table, Ruff resting his hands on his lap. The guards, stoic, silent, watched from near the door. "How on earth did you find me again, Ruff?" Sarah asked.

"Well, it took some doing, but I just asked around in Kit Carson. Some folks there told me where I could find you."

Justice looked at Kent with an innocent expression. The man's jaw muscle twitched with suppressed emotion. This, obviously, was the last thing on earth he wanted—a stranger walking into his nest, a stranger who knew his true name and was God knows who himself. Sarah seemed untouched by any of this.

Andrew, the butler who looked more like a hangman, returned with a boned chicken, wild rice, and a bottle of pale sauterne, and Ruff settled in to eat.

Sarah watched him with soft eyes which sparkled in the light of the candles.

James Kent's eyes were hardly sparkling. "What is it that brought you here, Mr. Justice?" he demanded impatiently.

"Well, sir," Ruff drawled around a mouthful of chicken and rice, "I wanted to make sure Sarah was all right. She was, in a manner of speaking, my responsibility, and of course I felt we were friends, you see. . . ."

"Money." Kent's interruption was harsh.

"We had agreed on a certain fee, James," Sarah said, although they had done no such thing.

"How much?"

"Well, sir," Ruff spoke up, "now the money really isn't that important. I'm just happy to see that Sarah is all right." He spared a smile for Sarah Kent and was answered with a frankly sensual smile of her own.

"Then you are welcome to share our dinner," Kent said, relaxing slightly. "Spend the night if you wish."

"I would appreciate that, sir," Ruff said. He dabbed at his mouth with a napkin, wondering how far to carry this fool's charade. "But there was another matter," he added, injecting a note of deviousness into his voice.

"Oh?" Kent didn't like it. No matter what was coming.

"It's nothing much." Ruff shrugged. "It's just that winter's comin' on, you see. I noticed you've got quite a spread here. Well, I was wishful of finding a place to hole up for the winter. I've worked cattle in the cold. Down in—"

"Impossible," Kent said flatly. "I've got all the men I need." He leaned back, removed a cigar from his gold case without offering Ruff one, and lit it.

"I only thought maybe . . ." Ruff said dejectedly. He glanced at Sarah and saw the pulse in her throat quicken.

"Justice is a dear friend of mine," the woman said quickly. "There must be a place for him."

"Sarah!" Kent stood quickly, his right hand clenched.

"Please, Jimmy," she said.

"We'll discuss it later. For now, Mr. Justice, I hope you have enjoyed your dinner. Ed will find you a bed in the bunkhouse. Goodbye."

Not goodnight, but goodbye. Kent's mind was already made up, but Sarah, after a conspiratorial glance at Ruff, followed her brother out of the room. Justice was left alone to slowly finish his meal under Ed's impatient gaze.

"You're a slippery one, ain't you?" Ed said sourly.

Ruff lifted innocent eyes to Ed and went on eating. "When you need a job, you need a job," he said and shrugged.

"If you land this job, friend," Ed said, "you're liable to be sorry you just didn't keep on riding." With a glance toward the door where Sarah had exited he added, "No matter what kind of wages you expect to be drawing."

# 10.

JUSTICE RUBBED DOWN his horse and turned it into the corral. Then he followed Ed across the dark meadow to the bunkhouse.

The men inside had a common tough exterior. Cold eyes and surly mouths. There was none of the joking you found in a working ranch's bunkhouse. No kids off on their first lark, no old-timers spinning yarns. Just tough, competent-looking men, most of whom had probably never seen a cow off a platter.

They met Ruff with a stony wall of silence. Whether something in Ed's manner tipped them off or that was their regular welcome, Ruff didn't know.

Grudgingly they moved aside to allow him to pass to a bunk where a rolled-up mattress and folded gray blanket rested.

"This is it," Ed said. That was the end of the guided tour. He turned and walked out, closing the door behind him.

Six men sat at a card table, and they watched Ruff from behind a screen of tobacco smoke. Ruff recognized none of them, but he would have bet a lawman would have known those faces.

When they stared at him he turned his eyes away. This was no time to start trouble of any kind. Without speaking he unrolled his mattress and clambered into the bunk, keeping his boots on and his gun near at hand.

He closed his eyes, and when he peered from behind half-closed eyelids a while later, they seemed to be paying him no mind. But Justice was in a bad situation, and he knew it. Maybe Sarah, ignorant of all her brother's schemes, wanted him here, but James Kent definitely did not. And it seemed Kent was a man who usually got his way.

If Justice didn't take the hint and leave voluntarily, well, there were always other ways.

At dawning they all rolled out beneath a somber, threatening sky. Washing at the well, which had a long trough attached to it and a dozen shapeless bars of lye soap on the two-inch rail which ran the length of it, Ruff glanced up to see an old acquaintance.

"Get tired of town life?" he asked Colly Higgins.

The man with the neatly trimmed black beard scowled at him, dried his hands slowly on a filthy towel which was tucked into his belt, and leveled a finger.

"You'll get yours yet."

Heads lifted to study them, and Ruff, wiping back his long dark hair, shrugged. "We'll see. Three of you didn't have it last time. Think you can handle it alone?"

Higgins took his courage from having six toughs around him, and he nearly came around the wash trough, but one of the riders, a lanky blond man with cobalt-blue eyes said, "Best watch it, Colly. Justice is a special friend of Miss Sarah, the way I hear it."

"So what?" Higgins demanded.

"So, if it comes down to who's leavin', it might just be you."

The blond man laughed, dried off his face, and stood, arms akimbo, watching Colly, whose massive chest trembled with emotion. "You better watch yourself, too, Dallas," Higgins threatened, but the blond man just laughed.

"Any time, Colly." He reached for his gunbelt, which hung on a peg attached to the trough, flipped it around, and buckled it; then, standing there, shirtless, head thrown back mockingly, thumbs hooked into his gunbelt, he laughed again. "Any time at all."

Justice watched Dallas swagger away, and from the corner of his eye he watched the expression on Colly Higgins's face. It was not a pretty thing to see.

Ruff turned away and, pulling on his shirt, followed Dallas to the grub hall. Smoke rose from the low chimney, and the smell of frying ham rose into the air. The wind was strong off of the mountains, and Ruff glanced that way. Then, feeling other eyes on him, he swiveled his head and looked toward the big house.

There she stood. Young, fresh, dressed in pale blue. Sarah Kent watching, waving. He lifted a hand and went into the grub hall, catching the envy in a dark-eyed man's expression.

"What're you, some sort of lover boy?" he asked.

"That's what they say, friend," Ruff answered lightly. "That is what they tell me."

There was plenty of food at breakfast and damn little conversation. Ruff had the feeling that they had been warned not to speak of business. Trying to broach the subjects of cattle, winter herding, and hay got him nowhere. He doubted that any of them knew much about such ranch work.

The big Mexican and his crew had come back. The man, called Paco, sat sullenly at the head of the table, his heavily hooded eyes bleary with a night's ride, his face shadowed with dark stubble.

"I am the foreman here, Mr. Justice," he said suddenly, loudly, so that several men dropped their silverware and looked up. "Do you unnerstand what that means, *amigo*?"

"Means you're the boss," Justice said in response.

He didn't let his eyes lock with those of Paco. He

adopted instead a timorous, hangdog attitude, and Paco grunted: *"Sí, that is what it means."*

After breakfast they all filed out into the yard. No one seemed to be in a hurry to do anything. Dallas watched Ruff with cool amusement. The blond man cleaned his nails with a jackknife as he leaned against the corner post of the corral. Justice went up to him.

"What's goin' on around here? When do we get to work?"

"When the boss says to," Dallas answered. He smiled, folded his jackknife, and walked away as if he didn't wish to be seen talking to Justice.

"Ruff!" He heard his name, heard a low whistle, and looking toward the main house he saw Sarah Kent waving. She stood beside a huge old sycamore, and he walked toward her, watching the wind form her light dress to her long thighs, full hips. The sky was lowering, and a chill wind had risen. Sarah's cheeks were red, her eyes excited, as he met her.

"It's all right," she said, her hands taking his. "I've convinced Jimmy. You can stay on through the winter."

"Fine," Ruff said, trying to reflect pleasure. Yet he wondered. Jimmy had his own methods of getting his way.

"What's the matter, darling?" she asked.

"Nothing. I was just thinking I wouldn't have much time to be with you. And wouldn't your brother mind—a common cowboy with his sister?"

"Ruff, you are a surprising man!" She laughed and stepped nearer to him, still holding his hand. "And what is this awful game you're playing, pretending to be ignorant, hemming and hawing all over the place! I know you, Mr. Justice. Jimmy insisted that it was no good for me to be seen with one of his cowboys, but I told him that you weren't that at all. I told him how elegant and fine you had been on the riverboat."

"Did you?" Ruff asked, wincing mentally.

"Yes. Ruff," she whispered, "I remember how it was with us on the plains. That horrible night the Indians attacked. I think about it all the time . . . it gives me the chills."

"I recall it too," he told her.

"There'll be times . . . it's a long winter we have ahead of us, and Jimmy will be gone with most of the men."

"Gone? Gone where?"

"I don't know, and it doesn't matter, does it? We'll be left alone, or very nearly so—"

"Sarah!" James Kent was on the porch of the house, some fifty feet away. He was not smiling. If he ever did, he hadn't done so in Ruff's sight. Sarah stepped away quickly, and, still looking into Ruff's eyes, she answered.

"What is it, Jimmy?"

"Come in here. I want to talk to you."

"In a minute."

"Now, dammit!"

"I didn't come all the way from Virginia just to be bossed around, James!"

"Will you *please* come here, Sarah. I've something important to discuss with you. Let Mr. Justice do his work."

"All right." She squeezed Ruff's hand meaningfully. "But you must come to supper tonight, Ruff."

"If it's all right with your brother," Ruff said loudly enough for James Kent to hear.

But it obviously wasn't all right with James Kent, former captain, U.S. Army. Nothing about Ruff Justice was all right with Kent, and his expression was dark, cold, and murderous as Sarah turned away from Ruff and with one last whimsical wave, walked to the porch, her capable hips swaying softly.

"Justice!"

Ruff turned to see Paco sitting his gray horse. He ambled slowly toward where the Mexican waited.

Paco had his sombrero hanging down his back. The

wind ruffled his dark, curly hair. His dark, scowling face matched the clouds draped over the mountain peaks.

"What's up?"

"There's a storm coming in." Paco looked toward the skies himself. "We've got horses up in Loggerhead Canyon. A very bad place to be caught if it snows. You're going up to bring them down."

"Alone?" Ruff asked.

"No. With him," Paco said, and those dark eyes flickered with amusement briefly as he nodded his head toward Colly Higgins, who stood waiting, holding the reins to a paint horse.

"All right," Ruff replied calmly. Paco frowned. Maybe he had been expecting a complaint. But a complaint, refusing to work, could get any hand fired, so Ruff agreed amiably. He was being set up, and he knew it, but there was no way around it.

"I suppose everybody will be out gathering stock," Ruff suggested.

"Could be," Paco answered. "If the boss says so."

The big Mexican drew his hat onto his head, kneed his horse forward savagely, and left Ruff alone. Slowly he walked toward the waiting Colly Higgins.

"You and me alone, it seems," Ruff said.

"Sure. You and me. Look, there's no hard feelings, huh?"

"None at all," Ruff said, and he believed that about as much as he believed it would just be the two of them up in those mountains.

They trailed into the high country beneath lowering skies, the wind rattling in the pines and lifting plumes of light snow off the mountain peaks above them. Higgins led a pack horse, and Ruff had fallen back, not wanting Colly behind him.

From time to time Colly looked around worriedly, as if he was having second thoughts about this. He didn't know Justice, after all, and if the man knew something was

121

up—why, it could be Higgins himself who was shot in the back and left up on the mountain slopes.

Turning in the saddle, Ruff could see the tiny rectangular forms which were the Kent ranch. It looked quite beautiful, nestled in that green valley. From this observation point it seemed that whoever lived there must have a peaceful, sober existence. Ruff wondered who had lived there before James Kent had come into this territory. And he wondered if, whoever it was, he was still alive.

The morning passed quietly. The air was cold, clear beneath the layer of mottled clouds. Now and then they found a horse and turned it homeward. At noon they ate cold sandwiches the cook had packed—thick slabs of ham between thicker slices of yeasty bread. Colly's eyes never left Ruff, and Justice wondered when it would come.

"How far now?" Ruff asked.

"Huh?" Colly nearly jumped. "Oh, maybe a mile. There's a teacup valley up here the horses favor. Good grass."

"Think we'll be back for supper?" Ruff asked, chewing his sandwich thoughtfully.

"Sure."

"Both of us, Colly?"

Colly's eyes narrowed. He held his sandwich halfway to his mouth. "Sure," he grunted.

But his eyes told a different story. They rode out half an hour later, following the winding, narrow trail up along the flank of the streaked gray mountain. This was all very neat. Ruff could almost hear the explanation to Sarah, see the crocodile tears in James Kent's eyes.

Sorry, Sis, but he just fell off that mountain trail.

On the other hand, Ruff imagined that if he came back alone there would be a hanging tree waiting. "Murdered Colly, the son of a bitch."

Either way it wouldn't matter much to Kent. He had no use for either man. Colly had botched his job in Kit

122

Carson. Maybe this was his only chance to make it up to his boss.

Kent was a man who used people and discarded them. He was the kind of man who would have been better off strangled in his swaddling. A murdering, arrogant bastard who would only continue to hurt more, to kill more, until he was taken down.

*If*, Ruff thought constantly until his head was dizzy with the repetition. If I can get close to him when there's no one around. If I can get him off the ranch. If I can beat his thugs out of Colorado . . . too many ifs, not enough how.

"Down there."

Colly Higgins had drawn up at a narrow bend on the trail and with a stubby finger indicated a small herd of horses grazing contentedly in a tiny meadow. "We got to go on down."

"Lead on," Ruff said without a smile. "You know the country better than I do."

"Yeah." Colly touched his tongue to his lips. The wind lifted the fur collar on his buffalo coat and twisted his horse's tail. Taking a slow breath he said, "We've got to go ahead a little way. There's a cut we can get down pretty easy."

Show me it, Colly, Ruff thought. Show me your short-cut. His eyes began to search the area more intently. He listened to the vague sounds the wind made, to the scraping of bough against bough in the forest. He was nearly sure now, nearly sure that Colly Higgins wasn't the sort to try this alone. There would be someone else up here. Maybe lying on an outcropping with a Winchester.

Colly found the mouth of a steep cut which looked more treacherous than going off the side of the trail, but he started on down. The rock was slick. The roan wasn't happy with the idea at all. But the chute suited Colly's purposes admirably. It took all of a man's concentration just to handle a horse down the sheer incline.

A trickle of a stream ran through the gorge. Yet at some times of the year it must have gathered enough snowmelt to become, briefly, a roaring river, for there were huge, horse-sized boulders scattered down the chute, making travel even more difficult, even slower. Above, the sheer sides of the gorge rose up to a height of fifty feet. Gray clouds shunted past.

"Hold up here, Colly," Ruff said as they rode behind a massive yellow boulder.

"What for?" Colly's voice was a snarl, but his demeanor changed perceptibly, rapidly, as he saw the big blue Colt in Ruff's hand. It was cocked and leveled at him. "What's with that, Justice? I thought there was no hard feelings."

"No hard feelings. Just to prove it, I'm going to give you my hat."

"Your *what*?"

"My hat. Brand-new one. Hell of a lot nicer than yours. Here." Ruff held it out with his free hand. "Put it on."

"Are you crazy?"

Ruff lifted the muzzle of the Colt, and Colly decided he wasn't so crazy. He put the wide-brimmed gray hat on and held out his own greasy black hat. Ruff glanced at it with distaste and put it on.

"You see, no hard feelings," Ruff said mildly. The wind was cold in his face. He could see the uneasiness in Colly's eyes, but Colly had no play. His pistol was under the flap of that big buffalo coat, his rifle in the boot.

"What're you up to, Justice?"

"Nothing. Nothing that matters unless you're up to something yourself, Colly."

"Don't talk in riddles," the big man said.

"All right. I gave you my new hat to show there's no hard feelings."

"Good." Colly started to turn his horse, but Ruff stopped him, grabbing the paint's bridle.

"I gave you something, Colly. Now you ought to return the favor."

"What do you mean?" he asked suspiciously.

"Aren't you going to give me something too?" Ruff asked.

"Sure, Justice. What do you want?"

"How about your coat?"

"You're crazy!" Colly was genuinely scared now, and Ruff figured he had guessed right.

"Let me borrow it then—just until nightfall. I'm cold, Colly. Cold as a grave."

Colly didn't like his choice of words. "No," he said sharply, but Ruff, shrugging, lifted the Colt again. "All right, all right!" he shouted, shrugging out of the coat.

"Shuck that pistol while you're at it," Ruff advised him. "And don't make the mistake of thinking you can draw and fire before I squeeze this trigger. A very soft trigger this gun has, Colly. It doesn't take more than a puff of wind to touch it off."

"Why are you doing this?" Colly asked, his anger returning.

"If you don't know it doesn't matter," Ruff said quietly. "But I think you know."

"You'll get me . . . you're crazy!" Then he shut his mouth, clenching his jaw, determined to say no more. His loyalty was pathetic.

"Lead on out," Ruff said. He stepped from the blue roan's back, his pistol never wavering. "And take my pony—he's good on a slope. I wouldn't want you to fall, partner."

Grumbling, Colly stepped down, eased past Ruff, and stepped into the roan's stirrup. "You're a son of a bitch, Justice," he said. Ruff was on the paint's back now, and he nodded, considering it.

"Could be, Higgins. It could be."

They moved down the chute, the horses' hoofs clattering against the stone, echoing faintly, ringingly, off the walls of the gorge. A fine drizzle had settled in, and it darkened the horses, made the footing still more treacherous. Colly was starting to sweat.

He swiveled around and looked at Justice with silent despair, and Ruff said in a low voice, "It doesn't have to be like this."

"I don't know what the hell you're talking about."

Ruff shrugged and let his horse fall back another length. He glanced up now and then at the silent stone walls of the gorge, but he saw nothing. The clouds and mist were low and the light was bad.

Colly, riding in silence, seemed to have a sudden change of heart. He drew up his horse and said urgently, "Look, Justice—"

But it was too late. The report of the rifle echoed through the gorge like the chimes of hell. The roan reared and Colly, clinging to the pommel, clutched at his shoulder wildly.

"Don't shoot!" he screamed. "It's me!"

The bullets had no ears. They slammed into Colly's body, driving him from the saddle to fall against the cold gray stone, already dead, his blood running down the chute in a slow, crimson rivulet.

Justice sat his horse, knowing that if he were Colly he wouldn't run. What would Colly do?

Ruff got down and turned the body over with his toe—not liking the feeling of playing Colly, pretending that the lifeless chunk of meat at his feet was Ruff Justice. Then he turned toward the rifleman still hidden in the drizzle, and waved an arm.

From on top of the cliff an arm holding a rifle lifted in return, and Justice settled in to wait. The drizzle continued, at times becoming stinging rain, and the temperature plummeted.

Finally Ruff heard the clopping of a horse's hoofs up the gorge, and he eased on over behind one of the massive boulders, waiting in the cold and rain for the man with death in his hands.

In a minute he appeared. He rode around the boulder, riding a black horse, wearing a slicker. It was the blond kid with the crooked teeth, the one from Kit Carson, and he had that Winchester in his hand still.

He halted, turning his head in puzzlement.

"Colly?" he called out.

"That's Colly," Ruff Justice said, and his voice was cold. The kid stiffened perceptibly, but he didn't turn around.

"Justice?"

"That's right. I thought you'd had enough in Kit Carson."

"Look, Justice . . ."

"Throw that rifle down, boy," Ruff said, and it was not a request.

"What're you going to do?"

"We'll talk that over after you've gotten rid of the Winchester."

The kid hesitated and then, from the twitch of muscles in his neck, from the tensing of his hand, through some primitive, nameless instinct, Ruff knew the kid was going to do nothing of the sort.

He turned, bringing his rifle shoulder high, but Ruff's Colt had already spoken. The roar of the .44 was loud in the gorge. It was rolling thunder, and it dealt death. The kid's face was twisted with rage and pain. His lips frothed as he tried to piece together a curse, as he tried again to lift that rifle. To kill.

But he was already dead. Ruff's bullet, centered on his torso, had been true. A heart shot, and the kid would do no more killing.

He fell from the panicked, sidestepping horse and thudded to the ground, landing not three feet from Colly Higgins, his body as still, growing rapidly as cold as that of the man he had killed.

"Now you stand steady, Justice," the mocking voice said from behind him.

"I forgot the three of you are a team," Ruff said. The Mexican's accent was unmistakable.

"One small error, Justice. But that is all a man is allowed, eh?" He snarled, "Drop that pistol!"

The rain was falling. The horses looked nervously toward the skies. The wind hooted up the canyon. Soon there would be three bodies lying in a cold row in this godforsaken hidden spot, left to decay and be torn apart by the wild things.

"I say drop it, *amigo!*" the man repeated.

Once he did that it was all over, and Ruff knew it. He would rather have a chance of taking the man out with him if he had to go. Four men in a row or three, what was the difference?

Ruff shrugged slightly, then threw himself to one side, rolling to fire up at the Mexican. But the other man was set, and he had touched off first. The bullet whistled past Ruff's arm, tugging at the sleeve of Colly Higgins's buffalo coat. And then everything seemed to slow, to focus.

He could see the smoke curling from the Mexican's rifle, see it whipped away by the wind. He saw clearly the Mexican's broken nose and two black eyes earned in combat with a door in Kit Carson. And then he fired.

The pistol bucked in Ruff's hand. The Mexican was spun around, tagged high on the shoulder by a shot thrown off target when Ruff's elbow slammed into the stone floor of the gorge.

The Mexican dove for the shelter of a boulder, clutching his injured arm, and Ruff took off. He crawled under Colly's paint horse, grasped the bridle and the stirrup, and kicked the horse into a startled downslope run.

Clinging precariously to the horse, shielded by it, Ruff heard the Mexican's rifle speak twice, three times. Lead whistled through the air, impacted on the stone walls of the gorge, spraying stone splinters, and then either the paint was shot or it slipped badly on the slick stone chute.

It went down hard, tumbling head over heels, its cry of pain shrill. Ruff was thrown free, and he landed with a breathtaking shock against the canyon floor.

His Colt clattered away, and his vision blurred. Through the blur he could see the paint, pitifully pawing at the air as it lay on its side, and then he saw the Mexican, rushing toward him, and he heard the rifle roar again.

Ruff scrambled to his feet, going down hard on one knee. The Mexican fired again, this bullet striking the paint horse, killing it instantly. Ruff dashed forward, wasting no time looking for the lost Colt.

He rounded a bend in the gorge, saw the water from three separate freshets merge and form a swift-currented stream, and with a rapid backward glance he leaped into it. It was swift, cold, frothing white as it roared on through the rain. Ruff gasped for breath, had a moment to remark the irony of it—these rivers would kill him yet—and then with mounting concern he heard the incredible thunder of water falling from height, in volume.

Looking back, he saw the Mexican, now far behind. He saw the soft puff of smoke as a bullet was fired, but he didn't hear the report, had no idea where the bullet hit. It didn't matter just then. The current was building, and he knew why.

He struggled against the current, but it was useless. High gray bluffs rose over him. The water, icy and swift, swept him along helplessly, and then the river fell away.

It simply fell away! The water cascaded downhill in a white, foaming waterfall. It was seventy feet down, and Ruff had time to look across the valley, to see the wall of black clouds, the deep green of the grass, the distant white spot which was a horse grazing. And then he was tumbling, spinning wildly through white water. He tried to break his fall, to regain some sort of balance, to land right.

He managed to get his feet down, figuring that was his best chance even if he broke both legs. Then suddenly he was immersed in cold darkness, the water writhing and churning, sucking him down into dark, cold depths to a place no one ever returned from.

His head filled with red fire, cold fire, and his lungs felt as if they would burst. The current raged against him, shook him and flipped him over, around, rolling him toward death.

Then, abruptly, he bobbed to the surface. Incredible! He nearly choked on the deep gasping breaths he swallowed into his greedy lungs.

He looked back and up, saw the waterfall tumbling down the canyon to the river below, and he swam toward the near bank. The current had slowed here, and with no difficulty he made the bank, dragged himself up onto the damp grass, and lay down, arms stretched out as the cold rain beat down.

He blessed the day his brother had thrown him into the pond to teach him to swim and cursed the day he had ever come to Colorado.

He had survived out of sheer chance. The waterfall had dug a deep basin at its foot over the eons, and Ruff had plunged into that instead of being dashed to death against stone.

He lay there a long while, not worrying about the Mexican. If the man was fool enough to come over the falls, let him. Ruff did not think there was another way down—that was why they had chosen that spot for the ambush in the first place, figuring Ruff could not escape.

He lay there for long minutes, his chest heaving with the need for oxygen while the river roared past and the rain washed down. He was soaked to the bone, battered and cold, so cold that he knew he would never feel warm again. The wind increased and the land grew darker. The rain washed down in heavy sheets, and sometime later the first snow drifted quietly downward from the leaden skies as Ruff Justice lay freezing against the cold earth.

# 11.

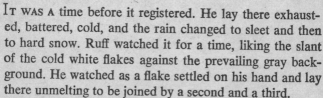

It was a time before it registered. He lay there exhausted, battered, cold, and the rain changed to sleet and then to hard snow. Ruff watched it for a time, liking the slant of the cold white flakes against the prevailing gray background. He watched as a flake settled on his hand and lay there unmelting to be joined by a second and a third.

The wind was strong enough even in this sheltered valley to bend the tips of the big trees to the east, to punish the cedar and blue spruce, throttling them. Lightning crackled brilliantly across the valley, and Ruff lay there, fascinated by it, counting the seconds until the thunder boomed, trying to remember the formula which determined how far away the lightning actually was. . . .

With a jerk he came alert. Dammit, Justice! He must have been struck on the head somewhere along the line. He was lying there, lying there freezing slowly.

"The hell with that," he muttered and started to get up, but his arms and legs weren't coordinated, so that he lifted his chest off the ground only to have his legs remain in place.

Finally he got to his knees. The snow swirled around him; his dark hair hung across his face. His mustache was hung with tiny icicles.

He realized suddenly that there was a very real chance of dying there. Never again to taste the lips of a woman, eagerly offered, never to sit a good horse in the wild country, never to sit in quiet contemplation of a vivid sunset. He forced himself to stand. The wind protested, rushing to knock him down, but Justice held his ground.

Stiffly he staggered forward, for a moment not knowing which direction he was headed. Then through the curtain of snow he momentarily glimpsed the dark forms of the trees beyond, and he struggled that way.

In the forest the wind would be cut. There would be wood. Yet his steps were ponderously heavy, his legs trembling, and the forest seemed to be receding, mocking him. The snow was ankle-deep and rising; the wind thumped him on the back, chilling his skeleton as his clothing froze on his back.

He was aware of the shadows first, and then he realized he was in the woods. His brain was working slowly, too slowly, as if the cold had thickened his blood and his circulation was slowed to a trickle.

What now? He had to pound on his head to clear his numbed thoughts. Lie down, his body pleaded, but Ruff knew that was wrong. *Fire.*

That was it. He still had his knife and the flint he kept in his belt, and now he scrounged around, digging under the pines where the rain hadn't soaked all, finding at last a handful of dry brown needles.

He moved to the lee side of a huge blue spruce and struck flint to the back of his knife blade. Nothing. He worked feverishly at it, and the hundreth time the golden sparks struck fire to the brown needles. They flared up, and Ruff immediately added another handful, then scraped around for twigs, tearing the water-soaked bark from them.

In ten minutes he had a roaring fire the size of a wagon wheel. The wind lashed it, and it thrust out tongues of fire toward Ruff. Quickly he stripped, hanging the frozen garments on low branches where they steamed with heat as snow sifted through the trees.

His teeth were chattering and his skin was blue. He placed his boots near the fire, smelling the scorched leather, and he jumped up and down, rubbing himself vigorously. Whichever way he turned, the side of his body near the fire roasted while the opposite side froze. He turned like a dervish trying to equalize things.

The snow, which had seemed lovely in his delirium, now seemed a weapon of hell. It lay heavy on the trees, and on the flats it washed down, obscuring all vision. Ruff fed the fire, danced his agonizing dance, and brooded.

Kent had sent him here to die, and he was damned if he would.

Kent swam in blood as Ruff swam the western rivers. Four soldiers dead back in the Nation. Bob Tuck dead. George Birch. What the hell did Ruff Justice matter to him? It infuriated Ruff beyond reason. Ruff Justice—just another meddler to bury. As if he wasn't unique, special, a living man with memories and tender thoughts. No, he was only a meddler. So much garbage.

Ruff danced by the fire. He leaped up and down like a savage, arms wrapped around his shoulders, working himself up into a fiery hatred, and the hatred kept him warm through the bitter night.

Dawning flushed the snowfields orange and deep pink. The few high clouds which streaked the morning sky were edged with gold. Justice had eyes for none of it. His rage was still hot, dominating all else.

He found his buckskin pants dry, stiff, and warm on the low pine bough and stepped into them. Then his boots—ruined by water and fire, but comforting to step into. The new maroon shirt Clara Tuck had given him was stained, and there was a rip in the elbow. Colly Higgins's buffalo coat had survived what was probably its first-ever washing intact, and it was only a little damp as Ruff shouldered into it.

Now what? That took some meditation. Deep inside,

the answer smoldered. Find James Kent and take him. One way or another take the man.

It was illogical, maybe hopeless, but his guts urged Ruff to do it. Do or die, they said, didn't they? Well, this was do or die.

He sat meditatively over the dying fire. Memory nudged him, and he stood, looking toward the empty meadow beyond the forest.

A horse. There had been a dozen horses out there. He had seen one even as he fell like driftwood over the waterfall. That was the first order of business—never mind the gnawing hunger in his stomach. There was nothing to be done about that anyway.

Find one of those ponies.

He walked along the perimeter of the meadow, keeping to the trees. The wind was fresh, drifting snow from the treetops to bite against his neck and face. He squinted into the sun-bright snowfield beyond the trees, watching for any color, any movement . . . and from time to time he stopped and motionlessly looked behind him toward the falls, wondering about the Mexican.

An hour later with the roasted boots torturing his feet and his stomach growling small pleas for relief, Ruff found what he wanted.

It stood hock-deep in snow, isolated, morose, and wary. It was the white horse he had seen from the gorge. The poor dumb brute was too ignorant of snow to paw it away and find the grass underneath. It didn't like the sight or smell of Ruff, and it took off immediately at a long loping canter.

He tried whistling, calling softly, and stalking it. No go.

He tracked the horse patiently for most of an hour, making a bad job of it. Ruff hated to admit it, but he was exhausted. Whether it was the cold, the altitude, or the residual effects of the gunshot wound, he was out of breath and leg-weary.

Then, by God, a second horse showed. A trim little bay

filly whickered from the woods, and walking that way, Ruff approached it. She came to him hesitantly, but as if she was glad to see a man. He was no less happy to see her.

After stroking the filly's neck and uncovering some grass for the horse and letting it graze, he slid onto its back, and within half a mile he was riding her as if she were a stable horse.

He walked her through the deep forest. The land was treacherous, falling away suddenly without warning where the water had cut washes over the years. The snow had covered up some of these, and Ruff took it slow, letting the horse feel her way.

The clouds had come in again by afternoon, and the wind was cutting. He eased up along a hairline trail toward timberline. He dipped into a gully which was running water, startled a yearling grizzly, and climbed to the crest.

There it was. The home place. Kent's ranch.

He decided to get as close as possible and wait until dark. Then with luck he could take a gun off one of the hands and catch Kent unprepared. And then . . . well, the hell with that. He had wasted time, nearly gotten himself killed trying to come up with a perfect plan. Now was the time to lower his head and bull in. You seldom get out of this world alive anyway.

Sundown was only a dull wash of color smeared against the smoky clouds. Ruff sat in the hills overlooking the valley, keeping an eye on the bay, which munched unenthusiastically at some low-growing brush.

He waited patiently, hunkered down on his haunches, watching the land grow dark. It was puzzling as hell.

There were no pony tracks across the snow-glossed meadow. The cook's fire was sending up no smoke. What in hell were they doing? Scanning the edge of the woods, he could pick out no perimeter guards, but it was dim and the guards were usually careful to conceal themselves. All the same, it almost seemed that they were barricaded in the big house or hiding in the woods, dug in. For what?

After dark when the wind was bitter and the snow had again begun to fall, Ruff led off down the long hill. He took the horse as near as he dared and then let it loose. It would wander to join the others of its kind in the meadow sooner or later.

Right then he was concerned more with people than horses. It seemed a bad night to die. The closer he got to the Kent house, the more foolish all that do-or-die stuff seemed. He wanted to live, like any man. Life was rich, flavored with colors, sunlight through the forest in the morning, women with lush, eager bodies and hungry mouths. But there was something that had to be done here, and he meant to do it.

There is a breed of men to whom self-preservation is all, self-gratification the end in itself. If they know what right and wrong are, they have so colored them with their own greed, twisted them to suit themselves, that they are no longer recognizable.

Ruff pitied them.

He moved through the shadows cast against the snow by the feeble, shifting moon and eased toward the corner of the bunkhouse. Nothing.

There wasn't a sound or flicker of movement anywhere, and he felt his heart slowly begin to sink. Taking a chance, he walked to the bunkhouse door and, with his Bowie in hand, kicked the door open.

The place was cold and empty. Half-empty cups still sat on the table, but the blanket rolls were missing. The place was deserted.

He recalled that Sarah had said something about Kent's pulling out. They would be left alone, she said.

This alone? He crossed cautiously to the house. The cold emptiness. He crept through the rooms. Nothing. Gone.

Every man jack gone, Sarah gone. He had lost Kent

again, and this time he had no idea at all of where he had gone. In disgust he sagged into a cool leather chair in the empty parlor, arms draped limply over the arms of the chair.

He sat there for long minutes, smelling the emptiness of the place, tasting defeat, his body sapped.

Stirring himself, he walked to the gunrack in the corner, broke the glass, and took out a Henry repeating rifle. He also found a display-case-new Colt and a holster. Ammunition rested in new green boxes in a tray.

Ruff loaded up and went to the kitchen, where he found bacon, the remains of a well-used ham, and flour. The ham he cut off the bone and ate as he stuffed a sack full of supplies.

Where he was going he did not know. How he would find Kent he had no idea; he only knew that find him he would. Find him and give him his choice, the last choice James Kent would ever make: hang or die where he stood.

He searched Sarah's room, expecting nothing. Nothing was what he found—no note, no hastily drawn map. The snow washed down outside, pasting itself to the window. With a last glance around the green satin room, a room which still smelled faintly of her—lavender, perfumed soap, and some more indefinite scent, warm, womanly—he went out, leaving the door ajar.

He rode out through the dark and snow, using the only trail out of the Cloud Peak ranch. As he rode now he found himself urging the horse on, found that his heart was beating faster. He had left her alone, damn him! Now he could make out the tracks of Kent's horsemen in the snow, and he followed them at what was nearly a run, cursing himself until he reached the fork in the road, and then he sagged with relief.

Kent had taken the south fork. The trail to Widow Creek was untracked snow.

Clara was something that could wait. Kent would murder her when the time came—just a bit of business to be cleaned up later. Her life, like Ruff's life, was unimportant to the man. But for now she was safe, although Ruff wondered as he swung southward how she slept these nights, fearing that the house would be burned down around her, that they would come with their guns and their hard souls.

He forced it out of his mind.

He had traded the bay for a five-year-old gray horse, a good strong gelding with a lot of leg and chest. The gray walked on through the night, the snow falling around them, the trees forming dark corridors.

At daylight it was still falling, but lightly. Ruff found himself at the open end of a long canyon where water glistened on the rocks. Below and beyond were long sagebrush-dotted flats, and a mile off a squat, snow-dusted town sat out the storm.

Here the tracks of the Kent riders split. Nearly two dozen horses had swung up into the canyon, while a single set of tracks led off across the flats toward the town.

Ruff swung his horse toward the town. There was no way of bucking two dozen men up that canyon. The horse moved easily across the flats and the town became defined, taking on reality as he rode closer. It was primarily an adobe town with two or three false-fronted frame buildings on the main street. Beyond the town another mile or so stood an army stockade, the colors rippling in the rising wind.

Ruff walked his gray into town and tied up in front of a saloon. He walked along a row of horses, finding one with sweat on its flank, its head bowed in weariness. He noted the brand and settled himself across the street in the shade offered by a general store.

He didn't have to wait long. Ten minutes later a man emerged from the saloon, stretched, and looked toward the clearing skies.

It was Paco, Kent's foreman. The big man looked up and down the street, got on his saddle-weary horse, and rode it to a small brick building half a block away. He went in and was gone for ten minutes. Then he came back out, swung his pony northward, and was gone.

Ruff walked his own gray past the brick building, read without surprise the small, gilt-lettered sign, "Bank of La Junta," and swung his horse out onto the plains in the opposite direction, toward the army post.

# 12.

•••• ◆ ••••

THE FIRST SERGEANT had a bulldog face and an immense set of shoulders. He nearly spilled his coffee as he rose from behind the orderly-room desk.

"Damn me! Ruffin T. Justice."

"Hello, Bill," Ruff said, sticking out a hand.

"What in hell are you doing in Colorado?" Their hands were still locked together. Ruff and Bill O'Gara had ridden some hard trails together in Dakota. O'Gara was all army, all man.

"I want to see your CO," Ruff told him.

"Looking for a scouting job?"

"No, I've got a job, Bill. It's just that it's kind of gotten out of hand." He perched on a corner of Bill O'Gara's desk and refused a cup of coffee. "I need help, and you do too—though you don't know it yet."

"Oh?" O'Gara frowned, forming two deep furrows between his massive dark eyebrows. "The CO ain't in yet," he said with an unenthusiastic expression Ruff couldn't read right then. "Don't expect a lot," he added in a lower voice.

Ruff inclined his head, his blue eyes asking a question which Bill didn't answer. They sat together, talking over old times, old friends dead and living, until the door snapped open before the wind and a first lieutenant with short dark hair, straight, narrow nose, and haughty, hooded eyes stepped in. O'Gara came to his feet.

"Good morning, sir."

"Sergeant," the lieutenant said in a weary mumble.

"Man here to see you, sir. It's important, I believe."

The lieutenant glanced at Ruff with evident boredom, gave O'Gara a look which indicated he didn't need his first sergeant to tell him what was or wasn't important, and then walked through to his office, closing the door behind him.

"What would Colonel Brooks have thought of that?" O'Gara muttered. He looked apologetically at Ruff and said in a low voice, "Lieutenant Campbell. He's green, and he's unhappy here. Just got those silver bars, and now he wants to trade them up for a captain's."

"I've brought him a chance to do just that. Listen, Bill," Ruff said, leaning intently forward. "This is no joke. My business is urgent. I've got to see the man."

"All right." Bill O'Gara rose without hesitation. He rapped smartly on the door to the CO's office and went in without waiting to be asked, his big shoulders set. O'Gara knew Ruffin T. Justice well enough to know that if Ruff said something was important, it damn well was important—to hell with the lieutenant's feelings. Maybe that was what O'Gara told the pup.

"Come in," O'Gara said a moment later, his bulldog's face pulled down sourly. Behind the desk, a copy of the *Denver Post* on his knees, Lieutenant Thomas A. Campbell glared unhappily at the tall man with the long black hair and drooping mustache.

"Sergeant O'Gara says you're army. Says you have a problem."

"I do," Ruff said, ignoring the tone of voice, "and so do you, sir."

"Explain yourself." He waved a hand toward a chair.

Ruff remained standing despite the invitation. "All right." He looked at O'Gara, indicating he should stay.

"I've been tracking a man named James Kent for General Hightower at Fort Towson down in the Nation."

"I know where Towson is," Lieutenant Campbell interrupted unnecessarily.

"Yes, sir." Ruff took a slow breath and let his eyes briefly meet those of Campbell. "This man Kent was a captain in the U.S. Army. Temporary paymaster, he took the opportunity to steal a payroll, killing four men in the process."

"What has this to do with me?" Campbell asked impatiently. He drummed his thin fingers on the desk top.

"What it has to do with you, sir," Ruff answered calmly, "is that the man is here. He has a taste for stolen gold now, apparently. He's holed up in a canyon north of here, and one of his men was scouting the La Junta Bank. He's going to hit it, sir. There's no doubt at all. He's going to rob that bank."

"You can't know that!" Campbell said, and irritation and uneasiness mingled in his voice. He stood, dropping the newspaper on the floor. Ruff's eyes followed it automatically.

"I know it. I need your garrison's help to stop it, to pull Kent in."

"It can't be done."

"Why?"

He rubbed a hand over his short, sleek hair. "I haven't got anyone I can spare. I've three patrols out now. A band of Jicarilla Apaches filtered over the Raton Pass south of here. They've been raising hell with settlers below Pueblo." He asked, "How many men does this Kent have?"

"Between twenty and thirty."

"Good God." The lieutenant slacked into his chair. "Didn't you look around when you rode in, Justice? I haven't got that many able-bodied men on this post."

"Then we'll have to go at them short-handed."

"We don't have to do anything!" He slammed his hand down. "Who says he's going to hit that bank?"

"I do."

"It's all supposition."

"As much supposition as saying the Jicarilla are going to make trouble. If you think those Apaches can raise hell, you ought to see what a gang of fully armed whites can do. Kent was biding his time in those mountains, running off a few herds, gathering men, and now he's ready. He's going to hit the La Junta bank, and when he's done with that it might be Pueblo next or Trinidad, but he's going to make a war all of his own, lieutenant. He's going to stain Colorado with blood, innocent blood—you've got the chance to stop him now. Don't turn your back on this."

"All right." Campbell took a slow breath and closed his eyes. "All right, Justice. What do we do?"

Daylight was already fading. A rapid, crimson sunset had been smothered by a new wave of clouds off the Rockies. The shadows laced, intermingled, and bled together. It would be soon or never. Hit it quick and make an escape into dusk, negating any pursuit attempt. Night would hide them as it hid other vermin which lay in shadowed places through the light of day.

Now or never. The bank closed at five o'clock. Less than fifteen minutes away. Ruff lay on top of the general store's roof, hidden by the parapet which ran around three sides of the roof, rising to a huge, square false front.

He glanced to his right, saw Lieutenant Campbell scowling at him, and turned his eyes away. If Ruff had guessed wrong he was making a damn fool out of himself.

The minutes ticked away. A saloonkeeper swept the boardwalk in front of his establishment. Two muleskinners loaded their freight wagon. Sunlight still touched the bell atop the old Spanish mission to the east of town. A dog barked off along the river.

Dust rose on the plains.

Ruff shifted his eyes, felt his hands involuntarily tense on the rifle in his hands. Lifting his head bare inches, he saw the horseman and then another in his tracks. A low whistle came from the soldier across the street on the bank roof. He had seen them too.

"Like old times," Bill O'Gara grunted, drawing back the hammer of his army-issue Springfield.

"I hope not too much like them," Ruff whispered. Bill smiled soberly. He and Ruff had fought side by side at bloody Red Buttes. That day a hundred soldiers had died before their eyes.

O'Gara hunkered down. They came on—a long line of horsemen off the dusk-darkened plains. Ruff counted them mentally.

Ten. Twenty, twenty-five. It was Kent, no doubt about it. There was no doubt either as to his intentions. Ruff shifted his glance to Lieutenant Campbell, seeing a frightened but determined young officer.

Ruff pressed himself to the tar-papered roof, keeping below the parapet. Kent's men would likely scan the roof-tops, and the glint of late sun on gun metal would spook them faster than anything.

Ruff didn't want them spooked; he didn't want them running. He wanted them boxed up and nailed down. From the corner of his eye he could see Bill O'Gara pressed just as flat as he was, see the blue shoulder of Lieutenant Campbell, the hat of another soldier farther down.

Minutes passed. Ruff heard the horses in the street below walking past. Stopping. The creak of leather, the chink of spurs as men stepped from the horses. Boots on the boardwalk. He chanced lifting his head just enough to peer over the parapet.

There were three men on the boardwalk. Others had gone inside. The door stood open. At the end of the street half a dozen men were posted. Others had waited at the far end of town. They stood, arms crossed, looking up and down the street from under their wide-brimmed hats. Tough, whiskered men ready to make their fortune or die trying.

Campbell looked at Ruff, and Ruff nodded. The lieutenant, pistol in hand, whistled, and the rooftops came alive, bristling with armed, uniformed men.

"Kent!" the officer called, cupping his hands to his mouth. Up and down the street, guns were drawn. Rifles and shotguns came into view from under the slickers of the badmen.

"Kent! Come out. There's no way out of that bank. No way out of town."

Kent wasn't going to come easy. A pistol exploded in the bank, and then another. A teller in shirtsleeves and vest burst from the front door and died crossing the street. A bullet slammed into his chest.

It was too late now. There was no stopping it. A window was smashed out of the bank, on the alley side, and three men plunged through it. A rifle from the rooftops barked, and one of them went down, clutching at his leg, as the others made a dash for the horses.

The Kent men in the street opened up on the rooftop soldiers. A corporal, careless or too eager, was tagged in the shoulder as he rose up too high. Ruff saw the marksman, a faceless man on a roan horse, and he settled the bead of his Henry on the yellow slicker front, squeezed off, and watched the badman tumble off, his horse wheeling away, wide-eyed in fright.

Six bandits rushed for their horses at the bank hitching rail, and the saloonkeeper who had been sweeping the boardwalk moved. He lifted his apron, revealing army blue pants and a double ten-gauge shotgun, which exploded, cutting down the bandits like wheat.

Two were killed by buckshot; a third, dragging a leg, made it to his horse. But he couldn't make the saddle, and the horse galloped off up the street through the crossfire, the bandit clinging to the saddle.

The two muleskinners who had been loading their wagon in front of the general store climbed into the box, turned the wagon across the street, unhitched the mules, and, using the wagon for a barricade, cut loose with a murderous barrage.

Ruff saw all of this from the corner of his eye. He had his sights fixed on James Kent, following him with his rifle as the guns around him exploded, as the street filled with smoke, as horses reared up and went down, as bandits, trapped in the street, fought back desperately.

Kent had burst from the bank, ducked low behind a trough, and came up firing. Just as Ruff settled his sights on the man a free horse had blocked him off. When the horse cleared, Kent was gone. Ruff saw him once more, behind another gang member, and he squeezed off the shot.

But Kent had been on the move; his lieutenant bobbed up at the wrong time and took the .44 slug in the middle of his forehead.

Ruff saw Paco, a gun in each massive fist, blazing away. He saw the soldier who had played the saloon-keeper go down, saw Paco pick a man off the rooftop with a careless, offhand shot, saw the big man bolt for his horse.

Ruff led him, fired, and had the satisfaction of seeing Paco crumple up and go down. But he rose again, dragging himself into an alleyway.

The blond man called Dallas was there with a spare horse, and he dropped the reins to Paco. Together they spurred up the alley and leaped a low fence, and with Ruff's bullets singing all around them, they broke free onto the plains. Cursing, Ruff returned his attention to the battle in the streets.

The roar of guns was continuous. A dozen men lay dead and dying in the street. One horseman had leaped the wagon barricade and escaped onto the flats, but the others were pinned down.

Three of them tried for the saloon but were met by a fusillade of bullets from the locals who were holed up inside. They died on the boardwalk, twisted and shattered by bullets.

Then it was still. The echoes died away slowly. Smoke still burned eyes and nostrils, but it was still. The world seemed empty. Dead. Nothing moved on the street below, and then gradually people came out, prodding the bandit's bodies, picking up their guns.

Campbell had lost his hat, and he stood on the rooftop, the wind shifting his sparse dark hair. His face was glowing.

"You've made a captain out of that man, Justice," O'Gara said softly. "And damn you for that." But he was grinning as he said it.

Two horses lay dead in the street. A third, injured, was put away by a shot to its ear. The last shot to be fired in La Junta that night. People milled in the streets, slapping each other on the back, hiding the bad cases of nerves behind laughter, jokes.

"Let's go on down and see what we've got," Campbell called.

Ruff nodded and walked down the wooden outside staircase to the street below. He didn't have to see. He already knew what they had gotten, and who they hadn't. He said so.

"Kent got away. We'd better get after him."

Campbell looked astonished. "It's damn near dark."

"Yes, it is. The sooner we start the better."

"We can't catch him."

"We don't know that until we try!"

"No." Campbell shook his head. "We've broken his back. He'll not try anything around here again."

"Meaning you've gotten the glory, no sense finishing

the job?" Ruff asked bitterly. Campbell spun angrily to face him in the descending darkness.

"Meaning, by God, sir, we've done what you asked! We've smashed this gang of thugs. I can't take a patrol riding out after that man on your say-so, and you know it."

"I know officers who would . . . the good ones."

The needling didn't help. Campbell spun away. He was going nowhere on this night, except into the saloon to accept the congratulations of the townspeople, to share some drinks, to return to the post and write a report of this glorious episode.

Ruff watched him walk away; a man in a dark town suit had his arm around Campbell's shoulder.

"This won't finish Kent," Ruff grumbled. "He's not that kind. He'll be back."

"But not to La Junta," O'Gara commented. "That's all that matters to Lieutenant Campbell."

"I guess."

O'Gara had a cigar lighted. Now he rolled up his sleeves, leaning on his rifle, smoking as the mountains to the west went dark, as the laughter and loud talk rang in the saloon, as the bodies of the dead were carted away by two old Mexican men who looked close to death themselves, so old and frail were they.

Ruff Justice was looking to the mountains, and O'Gara, knowing the man, asked, "Going after him, are you?"

"I have to. There's a woman involved."

O'Gara smiled. "I thought there always was when you were working," he said.

"I only wish. Like to go with me, Bill?"

"I'd like nothing better, partner. But I've got four months to retirement. It's not much money, but I'd like to collect after working twenty-five years for it."

"I don't blame you."

"I know you don't, Ruffin," he said, slapping him on the shoulder. "That's one reason I always liked you, son!"

Then with a nod of that bulldog head, Bill O'Gara was gone, ambling toward the saloon, where the drinking and warm good fellowship would go on all night with every bandit shot and reshot a dozen times, the exploits growing more heroic as the whiskey settled, blurring reality.

Ruffin T. Justice walked across the empty, bloodstained street, and with the sounds of music and laughter still in his ears, he swung into the saddle of the big gray horse he was riding and rode slowly from La Junta, lifting his eyes again to the dark and savage mountains.

# 13.

IT WAS A dark, frozen night. The snow had fallen for most of an hour and then the clouds had cleared away, revealing fields of brittle, diamondlike stars against a sky of black velvet.

The gray moved slowly up the winding game trail, the frozen snow crunching underfoot. The trees clinging to the sides of the mountains were black, star-shadowed. The three sets of tracks slanted upward across the open field, and Ruff followed them by starlight.

The odds had gotten better. Three men against him now, Kent, Paco, and Dallas. He recalled vividly and with grudging admiration the way the big Mexican had handled his guns. He would not be an easy man to take down. None of them, hunted, wary, cautious, would be easy.

Steam rose from the gray's nostrils. The hair on its back had frozen into tiny whorls of miniature icicles. The land was growing wilder. Mountain ridges, raw and barren, rose up and jutted out of the snow. The trees, wind-twisted and gnarled, clung tenaciously to the rocky slopes. The wind howled like hell's banshees down the long canyons. It was dark as sin, cold, bitterly cold.

The tracks Ruff had been following faded and petered out, crossing a long windswept slab of rock. His gray's hoofs clattered against the stone. The animal slipped, slipped again, and Ruff slid from the saddle, leading the horse across the icy, barren slope, rifle in his ungloved hand.

His muscles were stiffening; the cold had wormed its way into his muscles, to the very marrow of his bones, it seemed. Still he trudged on.

Toward midnight it clouded up and a hard sleet washed down briefly. The temperature, steadily dropping, reached zero and below, with a hard wind making it much worse.

Ruff's mustache was frozen, his long hair was white with hoarfrost. He moved on, slipping occasionally on the frozen, slanted earth, looking like a weird ice creature, cold, unearthly, inhuman. Except for his eyes. Eyes which burned hotly, all too humanly, eyes alive with determination and anger.

Two hours later the moon rose, a cautious, golden half-moon crawling apprehensively into the bitter, cold skies. The shadows crept out of their hiding places and stained the snowfields.

Now the massive peaks were thrown into sharp relief, and Ruff, alone on that barren expanse, watched, awed as they rose in pale majesty against the sky like stretching giants.

The bullet racketed across the empty slopes and the gray horse went down hard.

Ruff clutched at the reins, trying to stop the horse's helpless slide down the glassy slope, but it had gone to its side and was pawing at the frozen stone as it slipped downslope, its shrill, pathetic whickering loud in Ruff's ears.

Another bullet—from somewhere, Ruff couldn't even guess its direction—echoed down the long slopes as he cursed the vivid light of the moon which silhouetted him perfectly against the blank expanse of snow.

The gray was writhing in death, sliding away toward

the bottomless abyss at Ruff's feet. Its hoofs slashed out, and Ruff had to let it go or be hammered by those hoofs.

The gray, eyes wide, spun slowly down the ice-sheeted rock, tilted over, and was gone, falling lazily into the deep, shadowed gorge.

Ruff was off and running immediately. The bullets were being fired from far away, but they were amazingly close, and he wanted them no closer. He took a dozen long strides, found a narrow fissure, and threw himself into it, lying there, panting, hugging the frozen earth as if it were a warm, tender woman.

He waited for just a minute, catching his breath. The air he took into his lungs was like frozen glass, but soon his breathing settled to near normal, and then he moved on, not away from the rifle which had been firing at him, but toward it, down the long, weather-cut fissure.

The fissure narrowed and grew shallow, and Ruff knew he could go no farther until the moon either went down or was clouded over, and he saw no threatening clouds on the horizon.

He settled in to wait, arms wrapped around his knees, teeth chattering, Colt shoved inside his shirt to keep the mechanism warm, rifle propped up beside him.

The hours passed; the moon grew brighter, rising higher into the sky, then slowly, slowly descended. And all the time Kent was getting farther away. But maybe not. The terrain was rugged, the footing treacherous for a horse. Paco was wounded.

Maybe they were holed up for the night, just maybe. Too, perhaps they thought Ruff was dead. He hadn't moved for long, cramped hours, and they were far away. Their view of his activities after the horse went down might not have been that clear.

But he didn't feel inclined to poke his head up out of the crevice to have a look-see. He waited, the hours passing on slow, frozen feet, as the moon dragged itself toward the mountains above and to the west.

Slowly it dimmed and then eclipsed behind the Rockies, leaving a diffused golden glow to gloss the clouds for a few lingering minutes.

By that light Ruff eased up out of the crevice and worked northward, toward the narrow, snowbound gorge. He worked cautiously toward the rim, aware that any hasty movement might cause the drift of snow he was now working across to break free and tumble into the canyon.

He was in luck—well, it couldn't all be bad—for the gorge was not so sheer as it had been at the point the horse went over. It sloped away at a sharp but manageable angle. At least Ruff hoped it was manageable.

He intended to try it. Peering downward through the darkness, he saw nothing but snow. The drop was a thousand feet or more to the rocky bed of a roaring dark river. Once across the river there was a short, steep climb to a bench of sorts where no trees grew. A hundred yards across that and he would be into the woods. If he made it that far. Being an optimist, he planned his route across the bench and into the pines.

Then he eased on over. Once he had started, the drop seemed farther, the angle more acute. He tried it on his feet, slipped and rolled, tried again with the same result.

The new snow was glazed over with an inch of ice. It was slick and treacherous. Ruff sat down and scooted on the seat of his pants, using the butt of the Henry rifle as a rudder.

He sailed across the snow and ice, rushing toward the dark chasm below. How fast he went he couldn't have said, but the wind was cold in his face, the lines of hills, the distant dark trees a blur.

He tried to brake with the rifle, but it was no good. His speed increased with every foot downward he traveled, and he could hear the river roar.

Anything, anything at all, was preferable to another cold swim. He flopped backward, spread-eagling himself, clutching at the snow, clawing for anything which might brake his mad slide.

Finally he did slow, his fingers abraded, raw, his heart pounding. It was just in time. Rising to his knees he saw a sharp, fifty-foot drop-off, invisible from above, slanting to the river below.

He found a place to clamber down, feeling better about things. They hadn't seen him coming down. If they had, the bullets would have been flying.

He crossed the river at a narrow point, leaping from rock to rock, and crawled cautiously up the far bank. Taking his time, peering into the darkness, he threw a leg up, got to his feet, and sprinted for the trees. Each step seemed slower than the last; at every moment he expected the thunder of their guns.

Yet he made it. Panting, exhausted, he reached the forest and threw himself up against a bulky, wind-flagged ancient pine. After a minute's rest he began walking upslope, through the silent virgin forest. He forced from his mind the realization that if it snowed again a man without a horse might be stranded to starve and freeze up here.

The night was pitch-black in the trees. How long until dawn? He couldn't calculate it. He trudged on, trying to stay alert, fighting the cold, the weariness. There would be time to sleep when this was done. One way or the other.

He had gone perhaps a mile through the trees, crossing two ragged hills and circling a third, when he suddenly stopped. Pressed against a tree, as unmoving as the frozen rocks jumbled together on the hillside, he stood. Now, a step at a time, he eased forward, stilling his breath. He had heard, quite definitely, human voices.

"Damn her to hell." Kent, standing wind-rumpled, bulky in his buffalo coat, swore again and looked at Dallas. "How'd she get away?"

"She was there one minute, gone the next. It wasn't my fault," the blond man said softly.

"Should have tied her up."

"Let her go." The voice was weak. Paco lay on the cleared earth at the base of a tortured cedar tree, his head propped up on his saddle. The wound in his leg had bled copiously. The big man's swarthy face was pale now. His hair hung limply across his pocked forehead. His white teeth flashed as he grimaced in pain.

"I'm damned if I'll let her go," Kent said, turning toward his lieutenant angrily. "Where's Bobby?" he asked Dallas.

"Still looking." Dallas shrugged.

Four of them, Ruff thought, pressed to the snow, hidden in the shadows of the pines. Kent threw a stick into the now-cold fire. Paco shivered with cold.

"I can't go nowhere," the big man said.

"Stay here then, damn you!"

Paco's eyes were wide, heated. Sweat trickled down his face, cold as it was. For a minute Ruff thought he was going for his gun, but he was only trying to brace his leg, to get to his feet so that he wouldn't be left behind to freeze in those cold mountains.

Amazingly, he made it.

His dark, brooding eyes seemed to be fixed precisely on the spot where Ruff lay hidden, but in the darkness and shadows it was likely only illusion. Ruff tensed, his hand closing even more tightly around the rifle.

Now was the time, he thought. Now. Three of them, one wounded. He held his ground cautiously for a moment, and it was a good thing he had. Three more men rode into the camp.

"Well?" Kent snapped.

"Nothin'," one of the riders answered, slapping his shoulders against the cold.

"What about Bobby?"

"Didn't see him. Let's get the hell off this mountain," the newcomer grumbled. "If it snows, we've had it."

"And ride right down into an army patrol?" Kent asked angrily.

"There's no one back there."

"You're sure of that, are you? Sure enough to risk it?" Kent had the bridle to the man's horse. His face was set as if carved in stone as he glowered up at the outlaw. "Then get out of here, damn you. Ride!"

"By God, that's what I will do, Kent. There wasn't much of a payoff in this sure thing of yours, was there?" he jeered. "I hope the army does get you, you bastard. Me, I'm riding."

He glanced at the two men with him, and they nodded. Slowly they turned their horses and rode out. For a minute Justice thought Kent was going to go for his gun, but he let the men ride out.

At that moment a shrill whistle, far distant but clear in the cold night, sounded. Kent's head jerked around as if tugged by an invisible wire.

"Bobby's found her!" The three men were to their horses, Paco mounting clumsily, before Ruff could react.

They swung northward, and Ruff leaped to his feet, following. The sun was graying the eastern skies already, and Ruff jogged after them, the snow going to his knees at times. He didn't know what was going on here for sure, but he knew one thing—Kent meant his sister no good. The savage expression on his face made that clear.

Topping a timbered rise, he caught a marksman's dream of a view of Kent and his gang silhouetted against the orange sunrise, and he was sure he could have potted them all out of their saddles at that point, but that would alert this Bobby, and he couldn't anticipate what that would mean to Sarah Kent, and so he simply dipped back down into a shallow, sunrise-flushed vale and ran on, leaping a fallen gray tree, following a narrow, ice-fringed creek.

He could move up the hill a bit and see Kent clearly through the trees, but it was impossible for them to see him—or so he hoped.

Ruff was exhausted; his breath rose in steamy puffs. He must have run two miles before he saw the horses no more. But he could see their tracks engraved in the snow, and not a minute later he heard a woman scream.

He ran on grimly, circling wide. A jay screeched at him from out of a spruce and boldly followed him for a way. Ruff topped another hill and halted, getting his bearings. He heard a loud, cracking sound, then a man's guttural voice, and he levered a cartridge into the chamber of his Henry, easing down the slope through the trees.

". . . again, you bitch . . . if I can . . ."

Kent's voice, hot and loud, drifted toward Ruff, and he homed in on it. He stopped abruptly. He had almost stepped into the tiny clearing.

Sarah Kent was on her knees, her face in her hands. Kent towered over her, his open hand lifted. Paco sat his horse crookedly. Dallas leaned his shoulder against the haunch of his sorrel and unconcernedly built a smoke. The fourth man—Bobby—was watching intently, his back turned to Ruff.

"Now, where is it?" Kent demanded. Sarah just shook her head.

"You know I'll find it anyway. Talk, damn you."

"Kent."

Ruff's voice was low, but it carried across the clearing, and Kent's hand froze in position. Dallas had been licking the gum on his cigarette paper; now he stood motionless, his tongue still protruding. Paco's head came up heavily, revealing the eyes of a beaten man.

"Justice. Damn you." Kent laughed out loud. "You never give up, do you?"

"Not often. You boys want to let your guns drop?" Ruff asked quietly. He stood sheltered by the trunk of a massive pine, in a position to shoot but not to be hit.

158

"And then what?" Kent asked. "Hung by the neck until dead?"

"Something like that."

"The hell with you!" Kent dove, sprawled behind Sarah, blocking Ruff's chance at a shot, and sprinted for the woods.

With Kent's first move, Bobby had spun, dropped to one knee, and fired. It was a stupid move. With his back to Ruff he hadn't even known where his target was. His bullet sang off into the woods. Ruff's shot took the kid at the base of the throat, practically tearing his head off. Blood spattered the snow around the body.

Paco was going out anyway, and he knew it. He had calmly drawn his pistol, sighted it, and fired. Paco was good, but he was weak from the loss of blood, and his bullet smashed into the pine near Ruff's head, tearing a chunk of white meat from the trunk.

He never got a second shot. Ruff had switched his sights to the Mexican, fired twice, seen Paco's horse rear up and dump its rider.

He closed in, watching the horse canter free. Paco was dead, hit twice in the chest, his black eyes open to his last sunrise.

Ruff never stopped moving. Dallas was gone, Kent was gone. Sarah sat against the snow, her hair in her blue eyes, her face a bruised mask.

"Come on. Now!" Ruff yanked her to her feet and hurried her toward Bobby's wide-eyed roan horse, which stood tethered to the low branches of a pine. "Get up." Ruff had to help her. The woman was dazed, limp.

A bullet from the woods whipped past his head, and Ruff ducked low, yanking hard on the reins, heeling the roan violently. Another bullet followed the first, but by now Ruff had the roan off and running through the forest.

The roan was bogging down heavily in the deep snow, but they were in luck. Paco's horse, tired of stepping on its reins, had halted a hundred yards from the clearing, and Ruff swung toward it.

Through the screen of the forest, Ruff saw Dallas and Kent riding toward them, and he knew escape was not possible even if he wanted it. And he didn't. He wanted to take the man down, not run.

Glancing upslope, he saw a field of boulders where twisted cedar grew. "Up there. It's a good place to stand them off," he shouted at Sarah. He had to get Sarah out of their gunsights—that was uppermost in his mind. Sarah had other ideas.

Ruff gathered up the cut reins to Paco's horse, swung aboard, and was startled to see Sarah taking off at a dead run on the other horse—in the opposite direction.

"Sarah!" He glanced back, saw Kent's rifle go to his shoulder, saw the puff of smoke at the muzzle as the hastily aimed shot went wild. "Sarah!" She was riding hard in the wrong direction. Panicked? Mad?

He heeled his own horse after hers as another shot sang past his ear. Sarah had entered the woods across the valley and was driving her horse mercilessly upslope. Ruff glanced around, saw Kent gaining, and muttered a solemn curse.

He whipped his horse with his hat, bent low across the withers to offer a smaller target, and achieved the woods.

Sarah had ridden straight upslope, a killing run for a horse, and Ruff had no choice but to follow her. He turned in the saddle at the crest, meaning to slow Kent with a few shots, but the man was gone!

Ruff frowned and squinted into the sunrise, which had grown golden, brilliant reflected on the snow. Nothing. Kent and Dallas were nowhere to be seen.

Angrily, Ruff followed Sarah's tracks into the woods. He dipped into a small creek, splashed up it, and rode up a pine-studded hill. There he found her horse. Lathered, steaming, head hanging.

Sarah Kent was on hands and knees, digging furiously

at the base of a small rock heap. Her head came around as Ruff got down from the saddle and jogged toward her.

"Come on." He jerked her to her feet, but she fought away from him. "They're right behind us, Sarah. Let's get to cover, for God's sake."

"In a minute!" she shrieked. "I'm not losing it all now."

"Losing what?"

Her frantically digging hands answered that question in another minute. Slowly a small canvas sack emerged from beneath the covering snow. Sarah's eyes positively glittered. Her mouth worked soundlessly. Her breathing was rapid, excited.

Her hand dove into the canvas bag, and he saw the glitter of gold.

"You stole his money!"

"Yes!" She turned to him, still on her knees, holding the gold up so that it gleamed in the sunlight. The last of the stolen army payroll. New-minted eagles and double eagles. And for that the woman would risk death. Ruff looked down at Sarah Kent with pity. Her dark hair hung in tangles. Her coat was ripped at the shoulder seam. Her bruised face beamed, her unnaturally bright eyes searched Ruff's face. "Now," she panted, "now we can go—and live!"

"Now you can die." The voice was menacing and all too familiar.

Sarah spun wildly around. Kent, his chest heaving with exhaustion and emotion, stood there, gun in hand, eyes as bright as his sister's.

It was now or never, Ruff figured, and, turning, he went for his Colt. Sarah gave a cry and lunged for him, clinging to Ruff's arm as he tried to draw.

"He's my brother!" she screamed. Kent's gun spewed flame, and Ruff felt the impact of the bullet. But it was not him the bullet hit. The .44 slug had tagged Sarah Kent in the back, and still clinging to his arm, she slid to

161

the snow, her pretty lips parting to reveal a trickle of blood.

It was no accident, no accident at all. Kent stood motionless facing them, the wind working in his hair, and his mouth formed a soundless word: "Bitch." The gold lay scattered against the snow. A fleck of blood stained one brilliant gold piece; another lay in Sarah's white hand as she lay still, quietly dying.

Beside that hand too lay Ruff's Colt, wrenched from his hand. Justice took a slow deep breath. This was where it ended, then. Here, in the cold mountains, the free wind blowing the snow, the trees standing in dark, silent witness. All right. Then it ended. He would miss it all—spring in the high country, San Francisco, New Orleans at Mardi Gras, the soft breathing of a woman in the night, the shift of her capable thigh against his. He would miss it, but he had had a good run.

The shot was loud, thundering, and Ruff could only watch.

He watched as Kent, standing arrogantly before him, half-smiled, buckled at the knees, and went down. He watched as Kent, sprawled against the snow, died, his blood crimson against the whiteness of the snow.

"Bastard," Dallas muttered. His gun still smoked. He walked to where the body lay and, taking no chances, kicked the gun from Kent's hand; but the man was dead already. An unblinking eye stared up at Ruff Justice.

Dallas turned sharply toward Ruff. And then, nodding, he holstered his gun, and Ruff understood. *The joker in the deck.* George Birch had known somehow.

Ruff stooped, picked up his Colt, dusted the snow away, and holstered it. The two men stood in the clearing, not speaking for a long minute as the wind shrieked in the pines.

"Well, it's done," Dallas said.

"Yes."

"I never thought he'd kill his sister. Not even him." Dallas shook his head heavily. "I liked her."

"So did I."

"Dallas Boggs," the man said, extending a hand to Ruff. Justice took it, searching in memory for a hook to hang the name on. Dallas told him.

"My brother was Second Lieutenant Charles Boggs."

"Out of Towson."

"That's right," Dallas said. "He was just a kid. A few months out of West Point. Damned proud of that, he was. Proud of the uniform. He was the first one in our family to ever get an education, to make something of himself. Just a kid . . . The bastard shot him," he said, looking at the unmoving Kent. The snow had begun to fall from the high, rolling clouds. In hours it would all be covered with snow. The bright-red stains on the snow, the gold coins, the motionless bodies.

"I tracked him," Dallas said, finally holstering his gun. He looked to the skies and took a deep slow breath. A snowflake landed against his cheek and slowly melted. "I always meant to kill him, but somehow I never got the chance—until now."

Ruff crouched down. Collecting the gold, he placed it in the canvas sack. He stood there holding it, amazed at how little it weighed. The wind was hard off the north, the clouds rapidly closing.

"Where you headed now, Boggs?"

"Home. That's East Texas." He had gathered the reins to his horse, and now he swung aboard.

"Going by Fort Towson, by any chance?"

"I dunno."

"Do. General Hightower would like to talk to you. You can tell him what happened." Ruff tossed the sack of gold to Dallas, who shrugged and tucked it into a saddlebag. Then the blond man turned his horse and rode at a walk down the long slopes, never once looking back.

The snow had begun in earnest now. The morning, so

163

brilliant an hour ago, had gone dark, frigid. Ruff found the roan and mounted. What now—back across the plains in winter with the snows already falling?

It was done now, finished. Kent and Sarah already seemed less than human as the snow covered them, as their bodies stiffened.

Ruff noticed then the gold eagle still resting in Sarah's palm. He had forgotten it before. And now . . . he left it there. Let her carry it through eternity. She had wanted it so badly.

The wind picked up still more. The snow swirled down. It was no weather to be out in, and Ruff Justice kneed his horse forward, turning it toward Widow Creek.

## WESTWARD HO!

The following is the opening section from the
next novel in the gun-blazing, action-packed new
Ruff Justice series from Signet:

## RUFF JUSTICE #5: VALLEY OF GOLDEN TOMBS

# 1.

Sunset painted the walls of the adobes with a wash of
pale purple. The women walked homeward from the
creek, bundles of washing on their heads. Dogs yapped up
the street, and a nearly white half-moon rose hesitantly
into the sky. The tall man stood at the door to the adobe
house, watching night settle. The smells of cooking were
in the air, the sounds of domestic arguments, of children
shouting.

Dusk faded from purple to deep blue. The diamond
stars flickered on one by one and the moon took on
weight and substance. The door opened behind Ruff Justice and a hand fell on his shoulder. He felt the brush of
soft hair against his cheek, the weight of her head against
his shoulder. She peered across his shoulder, watching
day give way to night.

It was still warm. Along the creek a chorus of frogs had started their evening concert. A nighthawk dipped low over the pueblo. She was warm and strong and desirable as Ruff turned to her.

They wrapped their arms around each other and walked into the adobe, and Elena closed the door behind them. She was a dark, long-legged woman with a lot of Indio blood. Slashing dark eyes, ripe, full mouth, heavy dark hair which fell to her waist.

She was not a soft woman and she looked for strength in a man. Slowly, with the lamp in the corner burning low, Elena slipped out of her loosely fitting striped dress.

Ruff watched her admiringly, liking the thrust of her breasts, the dark, prominent buds of her nipples, the flat abdomen, the long, tapered legs, the businesslike hips of Elena Cruz.

Her gaze, proud and defiant, met his, and then she burst into a smile. A flashing, earthy smile. The smile of a woman who enjoyed her life, who reveled in her womanliness and in pleasing a man.

She smiled, and Ruff studied her wide white teeth, the pink cavity of her mouth, the twinkling light in her black, black eyes.

He stepped to her and put his arms around her, locking his hands together, feeling the involuntary response of the muscles of her back and hips.

"You don't kiss me?" she said teasingly, and he did. Her mouth was pliant, eager and ripe. She kissed him lightly and then deeply again, her body going slack against him. Ruff caught the scent of cinnamon-and-yarrow soap which was Elena Cruz, and beneath it was the faintly musky scent of woman.

He kissed her again, his hands resting on her naked buttocks. He kissed her small round ear through the screen of her hair, touched his lips to her throat, and then stepped back. He pulled his shirt up over his head and sat to pull off his boots.

166

Elena stood hip shot, watching her long, lean man undress with frank interest. His buckskin shirt he placed over the back of a rough chair, and now he removed his pants. She smiled to herself at the whiteness of his body beneath his buckskins.

He was not heavily built, but his muscles were clearly, strongly defined. There was a puckered, jagged scar down his rib cage on the left side, and below the collarbone were two silver-dollar-sized older scars.

Ruff placed his pants aside, and then he crossed to the lantern. Lifting the chimney, he blew out the wick. Then he walked to her in the night, taking her in his long, gentle arms.

They found their way to Elena's bed and fell into a tangle of legs and arms, their mouths searching, their hands exploring familiar, newly exciting flesh. Elena's breathing was rapid and shallow in the warm night.

Her thighs spread apart and he felt their soft brush against his hips. He found her breasts with his mouth and his head lay still as he kissed her gently, listening to the happy drumming of her heart.

Her hand rested on his head and stroked his dark, long hair. His head lifted and their eyes met, and in the darkness he could see her bright smile. This woman, so full of life, she who immersed herself in it, in work, in loving, smiled at him, and it was a smile which overwhelmed with its soft sensuality. Her eyes, deep in shadow, caught an errant beam of starlight, and Ruff, leaning forward, kissed her eyelids.

Her hands were on his abdomen now, slipping lower to caress and heft him, to feel the excitement in his body building to match that of her own.

She wriggled her hips slightly, sliding down in the bed until she had him positioned, and then she whispered into his ear, her words breathy, foreign, urgent.

He touched her and entered. Then, feeling strangely proud of themselves, they lay unmoving for a long minute, clinging to each other, Elena's words falling to a soft, repetitive murmur.

Ruff shifted slightly, his lips touching her throat, her breasts, her shoulders, as her fingers dug into his back. He shifted once more, and the movement brought a response from Elena. She too shifted, her breath catching slightly, and Ruff nudged her again.

Elena's hips began to roll slowly, to pitch and sway. The motion was fluid, and there was a power in her hips, an animal strength which was on the verge of exploding into a wild thrusting, an overpowering, demanding response.

She held back, her pelvis moving in tight, hard circles against Ruff, her eyes half shut, lost in sensuality, her hands clutching at his shoulders.

Ruff ran his fingers along the silk of her thighs, touched her abdomen, and sank to the softness of her crotch. She moved as if he had burned her with his touch. She thrust out at him with her hips as if in anger.

But it was far from anger. Those hips began to roll and drive against Ruff, swiveling and thrusting with the hard precision of a machine, with incredible strength, demanding, devouring.

Ruff clung to her, his breath against her ear, her hips swaying, her head rolling as an eagerness rose within her, as she urged him on, urged him to lift her to a completion.

He lifted himself slightly and swayed in response to her movements, their bodies moving in perfect timing. Her hands tugged at him, dropped to her crotch to touch him, roamed his back and shoulders. Her hair was spread out against the pillow in a dark, glossy fan. She had drawn her lower lip between her teeth and she held it there, biting down in concentration as he rocked against her, his drive growing to match the incredible pitching movement of Elena.

Her legs lifted and spread and Ruff felt her heels rest

against his buttocks, then lock around his waist as she squeezed and grappled with him. Her breathing was ragged now; her hands waved frantically and slapped at him. Her voice was pagan, her words meaningless, urgent phrases as Ruff worked against her, buried himself, split her, was met with a rush of fluid gratitude.

Their flesh was hot, perspiration-glossed in the warm night, and Elena gasped like a drowning woman, her body surging and twisting until finally, with a joyous, surprised laugh, she sat halfway up, throwing her arms around Ruff's neck before collapsing into soft surrender against the mattress.

She spoke gently, stroking Ruff's back, his thighs, answering his now-insistent thrusts with gentle pushes until she felt him go rigid in her arms, his long body tense against her yielding flesh, felt him arch his back and reach a long, trembling climax.

They lay together in the night, their hearts gentling, their breathing quieting. Elena's hands still roamed his body, her lips touching his ears, his throat, his mouth.

The night was warm, and it folded itself around them like a concealing, comforting blanket, and they lay together wordlessly, in deep satisfaction, until the first crashing sound.

The boot hit the wooden door of the adobe and it cracked. Ruff Justice rolled toward the side of the bed as Elena, eyes wide, sat up in horror. She heard the door give, splintering under the weight of many bodies, and she screamed.

They poured in through the open door, backlighted by the pale moon. Justice lunged toward his Colt, which hung in its holster from the chair in the corner.

"Get him!" someone growled, and the mob of men surged forward into the room. Justice was reaching for the ivory handle of his .44, his fingers within inches of it, when the boot lashed out and took his legs from under him.

He went down in a heap, heard Elena scream again as if from a great distance, and felt the impact of a fist against his jaw.

Ruff rolled away, aware of a crowd of peons peering anxiously into the doorway, of the armed, dark men hovering over him, of the figure of Elena, sheet wound around her, her eyes wide with fright.

He rolled away, kicked out with a bare foot, and caught one of the intruders on the kneecap with his heel. The man bellowed with pain and fell back, clutching his knee.

Ruff was cornered. He picked up the small table behind him and swung it in vicious arcs, fighting back the advancing mob. There was a moment's hesitation and then they surged forward.

The table caught one of them on the skull and he went down in a heap, but a fist arced in and caught Justice on the temple, a boot shot out and caught him on the thigh. The table was wrenched out of his grasp, and then they were upon him with their smothering weight.

Justice fired a short right to someone's jaw, caught a fist with his eye, and heard the bells began to ring in his skull, chopped out with another right which missed everything, and felt himself slammed back against the wall.

The big man was in his face, his sweaty bulk pressed against Justice, pinning him to the wall behind him. A ham-sized fist slammed into Ruff's rib cage, lifting him to his toes, driving the wind from him.

Ruff fought back the nausea, the dizzy lights which spun madly in his skull, and he kicked out, catching one of them squarely in the groin, but there were too many of them, far too many.

They had his arms and his hair. A gun barrel flashed in the moonlight and then slammed across the bridge of Ruff's nose, and he went to his knees, giving it up.

The room whirled, Elena's scream echoing endlessly as he was sucked down into the dark whirlpool at his feet, as the grim, brutal faces peered down at him and the night went explosively bright, streaked with crimson flashes before fading to dark, rubbery emptiness.

When his eyes opened again they had him by the arms and they were dragging him through the little winding streets of the pueblo. Dogs were barking at them, nipping at their heels.

Doors were quickly shut and dark eyes peered out of curtained windows. Ruff felt the blood trickling from his puffy lips. And then it was silent for a long while.

He awoke in the tiny, dirty cell of the Sonoita, Arizona, jail. He opened his eyes slowly. His cheek was pressed to the cold, hard floor of the cell. His head ached, and the air was filled with the sounds of a furious buzzing, like distant mad voices.

He rolled over onto his back. He was naked, stiff, and in pain. He had been kicked in the ribs and there was a knot on his head. He lifted an exploring hand to finger the lump, winced as he touched it, and let his hand fall away.

He lay staring at the rough ceiling of the cell, letting the dizzy confusion settle before he tried to rise. He managed it clumsily. He stood with his weight against the wall, eyes closed as the spinning began again.

When it had passed he moved to the corner of the cell where his clothes had been thrown. Dressing was only a minor anguish.

Ruff walked to the cell door and peered out through the small, barred window. The deputy, in a huge sombrero, was tilted against the wall on a puncheon chair. He looked up sharply at Ruff.

"Well," he said, "you got what you asked for, didn't you?"

"I guess so."

Ruff turned away and walked across the cell to the window. Gripping the bars, he looked out at the small

171

courtyard behind the jail, finding the source of the buzzing.

A yellow-flowering mimosa tree was alive with bees. One of them flew into the cell, angrily buzzing against the wall before it returned to the tree, flying arrow-straight past Ruff's eyes.

He walked to the cot which hung from rusty iron chains and sat down, holding his head. *You got what you asked for.* The bees hummed away the day in the tree outside the window.

They came for him the following morning, and there was a trial of sorts. The huge, mustached judge sat fanning himself as the prosecutor, who was also the sheriff, read the list of complaints against Señor Ruff Justice. There was no jury—no point in disrupting the workday of twelve good villagers. The judge heard the case himself, deliberated himself, and himself passed the sentence.

"Twelve years in the territorial prison at Tucson where you will have ample time to reflect upon the evil of your ways."

"That does seem like ample time, Your Honor," Justice said, but there was no humor in those cold blue eyes.

The judge glared at him for a moment, then waved a hand. Lifting his massive bulk from the chair, he departed for the cantina next door.

Justice was shackled ankles and wrists and seated in the back of an oxcart driven by the sheriff's slope-shouldered deputy. The sheriff himself rode behind the cart, shotgun in his hands, an expression of triumphant righteousness on his dark face.

They passed a knot of dirty, barefoot kids who broke off their game long enough to hurl rocks at the prisoner, and then they were out of Sonoita, jolting along the rough desert road toward Tucson. Justice had had only a single fleeting glance at the dark-eyed woman in the striped shawl who stood in the door to the adobe, watching after him.